"STARTING TOMORROW," PATRICK SAID QUIETLY, "it's your move, Merry. But tonight," he added, stalking slowly toward her, "it's mine."

Compelled by forces she didn't begin to understand, Merry met his gaze in the firelight, let herself be pulled slowly, effortlessly into his arms.

His Irish black eyes strayed to her lips and lingered there. "You have the most incredible mouth. I've spent fourteen days wondering what it would taste like." Spreading his fingers across her throat, he tipped her face to his. "You understand, don't you? I'm not willing to wait or to wonder any longer."

All bold strength, he slanted his mouth over hers and claimed it. Stunned, she arched against him, and he responded to her defiance by tightening his hold, lengthening his kiss, willing her surrender with a sensual thunder that dared her to resist. Caught up in the storm he'd created and the sense that somehow this was right, Merry wound her arms around his neck and kissed him back. . . .

D0816270

WHAT ARE *LOVESWEPT* ROMANCES?

They are stories of true romance and touching emotion. We believe those two very important ingredients are constants in our highly sensual and very believable stories in the LOVESWEPT line. Our goal is to give you, the reader, stories of consistently high quality that may sometimes make you laugh, sometimes make you cry, but are always fresh and creative and contain many delightful surprises within their pages.

Most romance fans read an enormous number of books. Those they truly love, they keep. Others may be traded with friends and soon forgotten. We hope that each LOVESWEPT romance will be a treasure—a "keeper." We will always try to publish

LOVE STORIES YOU'LL NEVER FORGET
BY AUTHORS YOU'LL ALWAYS REMEMBER

The Editors

Loveswept ® 637

DREAM TIDE

CINDY GERARD

BANTAM BOOKS

NEW YORK · TORONTO · LONDON · SYDNEY · AUCKLAND

DREAM TIDE

A Bantam Book / September 1993

*If you would be interested in receiving protective vinyl covers for your
Loveswept books, please write to this address for information:*

> *Loveswept
> Bantam Books
> P.O. Box 985
> Hicksville, NY 11802*

ISBN 0-553-44298-8

Published simultaneously in the United States and Canada

PRINTED IN THE UNITED STATES OF AMERICA

OPM   0 9 8 7 6 5 4 3 2 1

To my friend Ralph Palmer,
who dared me to take a dream
and make it a reality

Sue —
almost a
paranormal, right?
Love
Cindy

DREAM
TIDE

PROLOGUE

It was on the dark side of morning, the hour between awakening and dawn. Ghosts of midnight still drifted among the shadows as a slow-rising sun enticed an indigo sky to shades of lavender and pearly gray.

It was the hour when lovers turned to the lushness of each other's arms and indulged in the lazy heat of morning desire. The hour when dreamers, lured by the hypnotic pull of sleep, settled back within its silken web. The hour when realists, divorced from the secrets of the night, staunchly rose and faced the prospect of a new day.

Merry Clare Thomas, who until a few nights ago had never been a dreamer, fought the inevitability of dawn. Restless, yearning, she denied the realist in her that tugged her toward lucidity. Adrift in the scent of sea and heather, seduced by the romantic mist of nineteenth-century Ireland, she clung to her dream and her Irish rogue's dark, demanding image.

The thrill of his whispered kisses set her pulse racing. Fever-flushed, her skin tingled and burned as his mouth tracked across her body . . . slow . . . indulgent . . . hungry.

"*Please . . . just a moment longer*," she murmured, begging for time.

He smiled, approving of her low, needy moan. Lowering his mouth, he dragged her deeper into a dream tide of sensation.

She sighed, surrendered, then bolted up with a startled cry when the serrated buzz of her alarm clock wrenched her back to the twentieth century and out of her lover's arms.

With a frustrated groan, she groped for the alarm button and punched it off. Dazed, disoriented, she flopped back on her bed and drew a shaky breath. Except for a mild September breeze rustling the chintz curtains at her open window and the erratic clamor of her wildly beating heart, her bedroom plummeted into silence. And except for the hovering reflections of yet another wildly erotic dream, she was completely alone.

"What is happening to me?" she whispered as she raked the hair out of her eyes with shaking hands. He had been so real, she could almost touch him. So filled with energy, she could sense his essence hovering near. Even now, wide awake, she felt the residual heat of his hands brush across her body, the lingering taste of his breath on her tongue.

Shadowed and dark, he was as daring as he was sensual, a lover who gave more than he took, who excited and shocked, who was as addictive as he was elusive.

And he was hers. But only in her dreams.

Aching for both the dream and the man, she hugged her arms tightly over her tingling breasts and stared, bewildered, at the ceiling. *Why* was she having the dreams?

Everyone dreamed. She was no exception, she reasoned, grasping for some thread of rationality. But not like this. These dreams were different. They were infused with so much sensation, so much physical intensity.

Angered that she felt a little too shaken, a little too confused, she tried to think things through analytically. Was it stress? Maybe. Fatigue? Could be. Yet in all honesty, she knew that neither were viable explanations. She'd dealt with both before and had never experienced anything like this.

"Whatever the reason, Thomas," she mumbled, throwing back the covers, "you're a fool to let yourself get so caught up in them. They're just dreams . . . it's not as though they have the power to affect your life."

More troubled than she ought to be that such a notion had even entered her mind, Merry headed for the shower, determined to forget about them. And about the man who filled them.

She didn't want to think about the dreams today. They belonged to the night. Today, she had work to do. A business to run. A house to close on. Her own house.

The shower did the trick. The water was hot and invigorating, the stinging spray substantial and real and far removed from the erotic images she'd left behind in her bed.

Thirty minutes later she was ready for another day. As she closed her bedroom door behind her, she didn't spare a look at the leather-bound volume of nineteenth-century Irish poetry lying on her bedside table. She didn't look because if she did, she would be forced to acknowledge a niggling truth: The dreams had started four days ago . . . the same day she'd bought the book.

ONE

The cab smelled of smoke and dust and city. Patrick Ryan closed his eyes, slouched wearily against the seat, and soaked it all in. He'd missed the good old USA. All her scents, her sounds . . . even her decadence. This last trip had kept him away close to six months. Now that he was back, a cold beer, a soft bed, and a warm woman were high on his list of priorities.

The beer and the bed he could cover in short order. The woman, however, would be another story. While there had been some very special women in his life, there hadn't been one lately, and never one who'd been inclined to keep the home fires burning while he was away.

He thought about that for a moment. About the no-strings, no-strain relationships that had always suited his needs and his nomadic life-style just fine. Thought about the lasting kind of relationships he'd always shied away from in favor of his independence.

And as the cab wove its way through the dark city streets, he found himself wondering what he might have given up because of the choices he'd made.

It even occurred to him that instead of seeming restrictive, the prospect of someone missing him, someone waiting for him, unaccountably held a very real and powerful appeal. With that thought an unexpected and uncomfortable emptiness enveloped him. He quickly put it under wraps.

"Where is all this coming from, Ryan?" he muttered, choosing to be amused rather than troubled by the turn of his thoughts. Dropping his head back against the seat, he closed his eyes again and chalked it up to fatigue. He was too tapped out to think straight. Lord, he was tired.

Further proof of *how* tired hit home when the grind of the cab's brakes woke him a short time later. Shaking off the muzziness of a mind begging for more sleep, he unfolded himself stiffly from the backseat and paid the fare.

As the cab pulled away, Patrick stood for a moment and stared at the hulking Victorian relic looming over the caretaker's cottage he rented. Some people would have difficulty considering either of the century-old structures home. He'd be inclined to agree regarding the big house. Even in daylight it appeared uninviting and sinister. In this murky darkness it was just plain forbidding.

The cottage, however, was a different story entirely. Stumbling onto it ten years ago had been a stroke of sheer Irish luck. The cottage had proved to be his touchstone. His place to unwind. He'd done his best work here. Work, however, was not on his top-ten list at the moment. Sleep was.

Soft light and warmth from the humming furnace hit him full in the face when he unlocked and opened the door. Expecting a dark, cold welcome, he froze, instantly alert.

He glanced warily around, then relaxed when he remembered he'd cabled Jerry with his arrival date and time. Making a mental note to call Jerry and thank him for dropping by and warming things up for him, he tossed the keys onto the hall table and his duffel on the floor. The call, however, would have to wait until morning. He was weaving-on-his-feet-tired, and right now, nursing a bad case of jet lag and satisfying an escalating need to sleep it off was the most he could manage.

He headed for his bedroom. Toeing off his shoes and socks and stripping off his shirt as he went, he focused on the eight solid hours of shut-eye that came next on his agenda. Before he'd managed the fly of his jeans, though, a sixth sense warned him he'd stumbled into something unexpected.

A swift does of adrenaline shot through his blood and heightened his level of awareness. He flipped on the bedroom light. A hazy glow softly lit the room and cast midnight shadows over his bed—the bed he'd dreamed about for six long months as he grappled with sleep on a cramped, creaking cot he'd shared with cold desert nights and buckets of shifting sand.

The bed was empty now. The rumpled covers, however, revealed it hadn't been empty long. Patrick touched a hand to the sheets. The smooth, inviting percale still held the warmth of body heat. A woman's body heat. Even though it had been a while, he'd recognize the scent anywhere. Sultry, powder-scented woman. The fragrance permeated the room, drifting up from the bed, curling enticingly around him like a soft, seductive glove.

He glanced quickly around the bedroom. A woman's coat was draped neatly over a straight-backed chair. A pair of loafers sat tidily beside it on the floor. Before he could decide what to make of all this, a muffled noise coming from the opposite end of the house had him whipping his head around.

As soundless as a cat, he slipped into the hall and rounded the corner. His office door stood open. Soft light spilled out onto the hall carpet. He quietly approached the door, then sized up the room—and the woman rifling through his bookcase. Puzzled, intrigued, he checked another surge of adrenaline and watched her in silence.

She was a busy little body, rummaging through his library of books, trading one for another, as if having trouble deciding which book was worth the investment of her time. She didn't have a clue that she had an audience. And *he* didn't have a clue as to who she was.

The only thing he knew with any certainty was that she was, without qualifiers, a beauty.

He studied her profile as she tucked a skein of short chestnut-brown hair behind her ear. His scowl relaxed as she thumbed through a book, set it back with a sigh, and reached for another. For some reason it amused him that she was being so picky. So did the creases of annoyance that furrowed the aristocratic slope of her brow.

What she was looking for was beyond him. And frankly, if she was here with crime on her mind, she'd picked a helluva way to dress for it. She was wearing a white satin nightshirt and—judging by the play of dim light and shifting shadows—little else save that seductive scent that was still wreaking havoc with his hormones. The short nightshirt showed plenty of long leg and bare skin of a soft olive hue that hinted at judicious encounters with the sun and fostered a curiosity in Patrick to know if she was the same honeyed tan all over. Along the same line, he concluded that if the curves gently filling out the nightshirt fulfilled their promise, she had a body that could entice a monk from his vows of celibacy.

He was no monk. And it had been a long time since he'd had anything to warm his blood but a hot desert sun.

As he stood there wrestling with the stirrings of a healthy libido and the demands of common sense, he finally realized fatigue was coloring his better judgment. The inescapable truth was, the woman was not an invited guest. It was past time he found out what she was doing here.

"You'll like that one," he said very softly.

If he'd been giving points for reactions, he'd have rated hers at the top of the scale. The scream that ripped from her throat was a beaut. She jumped well too. And when she spun around to face him, he could have sworn from the look on her face that she felt *she* was the one whose space was being violated. She pressed against the bookcase wall, her eyes watchful as she glanced from him to the door, obviously contemplating escape.

He wasn't about to let her go.

"Of course, I could be wrong," he added, bending to pick up the book that had shot out of her hand and skidded across the floor to his feet. He frowned from the book to her. "But it wasn't really necessary to fling it at me, love. A simple 'no, I don't think I'll like it' would have done the trick."

He saw something in her eyes then that gave him pause. Something as soft and fragile as the satin nightshirt she was wearing. Something that made him feel like a heel for deliberately frightening her and stirred both a primitive arousal and a protective instinct he hadn't realized was so strong inside him.

Just when he'd decided there were no more firsts left to experience, he mused, too tired to dodge a dose of cynicism.

Puzzled that he'd let his emotions outdistance his logic again, he tossed the book onto his desk and advanced several deliberately threatening steps toward her.

She seemed to mold herself even closer to the wall.

"Th-this house is protected by silent alarms," she told him jerkily. "The police will be here any . . . any second. If you leave now . . . you can still get away."

Patrick suddenly felt as if he'd entered a movie theater in the middle of a complicated film. She was actually warning him out of his own house, and with a bald-face lie. The cottage didn't have security any more sophisticated than a dead bolt and a key tucked under a downspout.

"Get away?" he said. Though he knew he was frightening her, he moved even closer.

Eyes wide, she nodded. "There's still time before the police get here. Just go. I don't have any money—if they catch you here, it'll all be for nothing."

He stared at her in bewildered fascination. This close, she was even more enticing than at first glance. This close, the scent that clung but did not cloy eddied along his nerve endings in a rush of sexual heat. This close, he could see that the heather gray of her eyes was shot through with vivid specks of forest green. And with a very real and pressing fear she was trying valiantly to hide.

"In the first place, love," he began, giving in to a puzzling desire to put her at ease, "*if* there were an alarm system—which, by the way, there isn't—and *if* there is a need for anyone to 'get away,' as you so quaintly put it, I'm thinking you might be a bit confused about who that someone is . . . unless, of course, you can think of a reason I'd want to 'get away' from my own home."

"Y-your home?" she asked in a breathless little whisper that not only made it difficult to maintain a scowl, but prompted the return of those deep, sensual stirrings he'd been fighting since her scent had wrapped around him in his bedroom.

"You mean you . . . ?"

"Live here," he supplied helpfully when she faltered.

The panic in her eyes gave way to relief; relief yielded quickly to remorse.

"Oh, dear," she murmured.

"Actually, it's Patrick. Patrick Ryan. But if you'd rather call me 'dear,' I think I can live with it."

Both his words and his delivery were deliberate attempts at provocation. To his delight, she rose swiftly to the bait. Fire brightened her eyes. Glorious, gutsy fire, and in that moment he strongly suspected there were many things she'd like to call him . . . none of them endearments.

He grinned.

She didn't much care for that either.

Lord, she was a fine-looking woman. Somehow she managed to appear soft and feminine, determined and angry, and entirely too vulnerable, all at once. Sultry sex appeal shimmered with every breath she drew. And every breath she drew emphasized the shape of generous breasts pressing arrestingly against her nightshirt, just a deep breath away from his bare chest. It occurred to him then that if he lived to be a hundred, he'd never think of white as virginal again.

He couldn't help himself. He touched her shoulder, then suffered another swift and deadly assault on his senses. He quickly dropped his hand away from smooth white satin that covered warm, supple flesh.

"I sense you might be having a little difficulty with this, love. You can relax, you know. I'm not going to hurt you, but the fact is, while I'm a patient man, I would like some answers. I think I've waited long enough, don't you?"

Prompted by the uncertainty in her eyes, he backed away. But only a little. "Let's make it easy for you then. Why don't you begin, as they say, at the beginning."

The beginning. Merry closed her eyes and thought back to the beginning. Was it really only a few days ago that she was in control of her life and accountable for her actions?

Accountability didn't seem to be her strong suit anymore. So why, she asked herself fatalistically, was she surprised to find herself in this fix? It was the perfect twist to the roller-coaster ride her life had become.

She looked up at the man standing in such uncomfortably close proximity and wondered just how much trouble she was in. It wasn't just the fact that he'd surprised the breath out of her that bothered her; it was the fact that she should be afraid of him and wasn't. Not really. Instead, she felt an intense physical awareness of him as a man, and a niggling sensation that she knew him. Which was impossible. She'd never seen him before—she was sure of it. Still, she took a longer look.

He wasn't a young man. But neither was he old. The deep creases fanning out from his dark eyes suggested he was on the long side of thirty and that he had an easy smile—like the one directed at her now. His hair was dark, thick and lush, as black and beguiling as his eyes. The ruddy bronze of his skin indicated he'd spent hours in the sun. In fact, every inch of the approximately six feet of him that she could see—and she could see plenty—was toned and tan.

A prickle of awareness reminded her that he was waiting for an explanation. And that he was watching her—with entirely too much amusement, and, if she wasn't mistaken, with entirely too much interest.

His wide, expressive mouth hinted at just enough rascal to entice, just enough sincerity to compel. And far too much sex appeal for his own good. Or hers, she admitted, angered and amazed that she was reacting to a virtual stranger on such a level.

And he was a stranger, she told herself again, convincing herself she'd never seen him before. That certainty aside, however, she did recognize his name. He was the Irish tenant the real estate agent had told her about. She supposed she owed him an explanation.

"Do you have any identification?" she asked, stalling for time.

He gave her an incredulous look before breaking into another infuriatingly arrogant grin. "Absolutely," he said. "And to demonstrate what a sport I am, I'll show you mine if you show me yours.

"What, love?" he asked, all innocence and light when she deepened her scowl. "Did I breach some sort of breaking-and-entering etiquette? Forgive me, but since you're the intruder, I assumed I was entitled to a little latitude. Maybe you'd prefer that I simply frisk you instead," he added, giving her a thorough and blatantly provocative once-over.

"You wouldn't dare."

"Oh, but I would. With great pleasure and without hesitation. Surely you can appreciate where I'm coming from on this. It's my house; I feel compelled to make the house rules. And one of those rules is that whether you like it or not, I'm going to have to insist that you answer questions, not ask them. Keeping that in mind, along with the fact that sleep deprivation tends to make me cranky—and I'm sadly in need of sleep, by the way—why don't we start with your name?"

Realizing there was no escaping it any longer, she lifted her chin. "Merry," she gritted out between clenched teeth, then added the qualifier that came automatically after so many years of explanation, "with an *e* and two *r*'s."

"Merry," he repeated, and with a slow, studied motion, touched a hand to her hair. The gentleness of his strangely comforting caress kept her from flinching. Just the opposite. She stood mesmerized as he looked from her hair to her face.

"Pretty name, Merry. Old-fashioned." His soft, seductive rasp made her acutely aware of his maleness and all that bare skin so close to her. "Makes a man wonder," he added as his gaze dropped and lingered on the front of her nightshirt before lazily meeting her eyes again, "why such a pretty woman with such an old-fashioned name would resort to sneaking into a man's house and into his bed uninvited."

"I did not *sneak* into your house . . . or your bed," she managed, breaking the spell he'd been weaving.

"No?" His tone hinted that he wished otherwise.

"No," she whispered, thinking about the bed in question and remembering the inexplicable sense of familiarity that had swamped her when she'd first slipped between his sheets.

A seductive smile tugged at one corner of his mouth. "What would you call it, then?"

It would be so easy to react to that smile. She quickly squashed the thought. "Rotten timing."

He laughed.

She didn't see anything even marginally funny. About his reactions or hers. It was time to provide a little perspective. "Look, Mr. Ryan, this is going to be a bit hard for you to swallow, but the truth is, technically, this is my house, not yours."

That took him aback, but only for a moment. "Your house?"

"As of yesterday."

"I know I've been gone of late, love, but there's a

little matter of a lease. I recall having recently signed one."

"Yes, well, I know all about your lease. As your new landlord, I made it my business to know."

"Landlord?"

She nodded in triumph, and he looked momentarily stunned. Her victory, however, was short-lived.

"Now wait . . ." His grin returned as he angled his chin in the direction of the big house. "Are you telling me that you actually bought that hulking old relic next door?"

"That hulking old *relic*," she began testily, "and this cottage—which I'd like to remind you goes with the property—now belong to me."

He shook his head, his dark eyes taking on a decidedly amused twinkle. "So Max found another live one, did he?"

The Max he was referring to was Max Stoner, of Stoner Realty. And she didn't like one little bit the inference that she'd been duped.

"Live one?" she echoed sarcastically. "If anyone's been taken advantage of here, Mr. Ryan, it's Max. I know a good buy and a solid investment when I see one. This cottage is steady income-producing property. And since I'll be moving in next door, I can keep an eye on my investment."

"Did you say you're moving in? To the big house?"

She didn't think she liked the look in his eyes. It was sort of a "Well, well, what have we here," look that was pensive and amused and concerned all at the same time.

"Do you have a problem with that?"

"No," he said slowly. His grin returned as he gave her nightshirt another slow, thorough once-over. "No problem. Just makes me wonder, though, if the next thing you're going to tell me is that you're here to collect your rent."

Attitude. The man was full of it. Merry sighed deeply. She'd like to tell him what he could do with both his attitude and his flirty smile. Even better, she'd like to rub that smirk off his face with coarse sandpaper.

Never mind his Irish black eyes and sexy, rascal grin. Never mind the dark stubble of beard darkening his strong jaw or the deep tan that turned his skin to burnished gold or the fact that everything about him was physically compelling. And never mind that she felt far too susceptible to the entire package.

She was doing it again, she realized suddenly. She was cataloguing his features, and he'd caught her at it. Feeling her face redden, she made a vague, expansive gesture in the general vicinity of his chest. "Look, do you suppose you could find it in you to put on a shirt or something?"

"Well, I would," he said, not even trying to tone down his grin, "but I wouldn't want you to feel under-dressed."

She glared at him. "You really find this amusing, don't you."

"Yeah. I do."

"Fine," she began stiffly, "but I find myself growing very weary of your smirks and innuendos."

"And, sweet Merry, I find myself just plain weary. Before we put this to bed, though, love"—he paused and graced her with a suggestive drop of his eyes— "even if what you're telling me is true, it still doesn't explain what you're doing here tonight."

"What about you?" she sputtered, figuring she was entitled to a few answers of her own. "Max told me you were off in the Far East on some great adventure—that you were *always* off on some great adventure," she added, aware that the accusation in her voice had intensified a notch, along with her frustration. "You aren't supposed to be within a continent of the East Coast—let alone this cottage."

He shrugged. "Plans change."

No kidding, she thought, wishing she could rewind the tape and start this day over again. Since an explanation really was in order, she tried to figure out the simplest one.

She'd been so excited. From the moment she'd seen the ancient three-story Victorian mansion and the quaint caretaker's cottage that came with the property, she'd been itching to put her mark on it. Since finalizing the purchase the day before, she hadn't been able to stay away.

Armed with cleaning supplies, she'd started her great adventure by cleaning from morning to well past 10:00 P.M. Thoroughly exhausted, she'd slipped into her nightshirt and her sleeping bag and fallen asleep, planning on an early start again the next morning.

What she hadn't planned on was the furnace going out around midnight.

She could not tolerate the cold. And since her apartment was clear across town and it was the dead of night, she'd chosen the most logical option. According to Max, her tenant was gone and not expected to be back anytime soon. Counting on that, she'd let herself inside the cottage and turned on the heat. On edge and unable to sleep, she'd wandered from room to room until she'd found the library. That's where Patrick Ryan had found her.

As concisely as she could manage, she grudgingly filled him in.

"I'm so glad you find it entertaining," she muttered, his dancing eyes making his reaction glaringly obvious.

"Entertaining. Interesting. But I'm afraid I'll have to take issue with your assessment of the timing, love." He touched a hand to her shoulder. "It's not rotten at all. In fact, I think your timing is perfect."

Some people were natural touchers. While Patrick Ryan seemed to fall into that category, the way he did it suggested that his purpose was to keep her rattled and off-balance.

"Well," she said, attempting to pull herself together, "I'll just get my coat and get out of your hair."

"Whoa." Both hands found a home on her shoulders and squeezed lightly. "My mother raised a gentleman, and no gentleman would let a lady go out in the cold. You take the bed. The sofa will do me just fine."

If there was a gentleman lurking behind those devil-black eyes of his, she thought to herself, he was hiding far back in the shadows. However, while she would have preferred to believe he had a black heart to complete the picture, she reluctantly admitted she also saw a hint of kindness shining through as he watched her waver.

In the end, it didn't matter what she thought, because he didn't give her a chance to argue. He took her hand and tugged her with him down the hall and into the bedroom.

After rummaging around in the closet he turned with his arms full of pillow and blanket. He caught her glancing in the direction of her coat and shoes.

"I'll close the door if it will make you feel better."

The sensual dare that laced through his words stiffened her spine. She abruptly sat down on the bed.

He smiled. "Sleep tight, love," he said. Reading the look she gave him, he closed the door behind him.

TWO

Patrick had thirty-eight years of hard living behind him. His adventures had taken him all over the world—close to the edge, in fact, on several occasions. His life history was filled with events most people only read about, and as Irish luck would have it, many people were more than happy to *pay* to read about. The obscene amount of money he'd made fictionalizing his exploits for the past ten years no longer amazed him.

Given that history, it took a lot to surprise him. It took even more to shock him. Yet a satin-wrapped bundle of sultry, visibly irritated woman had managed to do both. That she had also managed to intrigue him was a credit to her rich heather eyes, her soft, kissable mouth, and that smooth tanned skin that made him think of warm ocean breezes and lazy tropical midnights.

He stared at his closed bedroom door and suppressed a groan. No doubt about it: He was going to get to know her better. Tomorrow. If he didn't get horizontal soon, he was going to pass out standing up.

After settling wearily onto the sofa, he stared into the dark, imagining how she must look lying in his bed, her chestnut-colored hair feathering across his pillow. He felt a sudden tightening in his gut when he flashed on a vividly erotic picture of his hands tangled in the fine, silky strands.

One image drifted into another . . . her soft body snuggled up next to his. Her sleepy sighs as she wrapped herself around him as if he were the mattress and she a fitted sheet—a satin sheet, smooth, supple, sensual. Her breath falling sleep-sweet and fragile against his jaw. Her breasts, full and yielding, pressed against his chest. Her long, smooth legs tangled with his.

Steeped in thoughts of lush, fragrant flesh and shared body heat, he fell asleep aching to know what it would be like to bury himself so deep inside her that it would take an act of Congress to get him out. And suspecting that if a man like him ever had reason to question his choice of life-style, the answers just might lie with a woman like her.

On the other side of the bedroom door, Merry crawled hesitantly into bed—his bed. She wouldn't sleep. She couldn't sleep, she told herself. Not with him lying out there on the sofa. She'd just have to suffer through until daylight and then get out of here.

Only somehow, it didn't quite work that way. Against her will, her eyes grew heavy and her resolve to stay awake weakened.

Only for a few minutes' she promised herself. She'd just catch a few minutes' sleep. She turned off the light and closed her eyes. The cool brush of the night breeze shivered against her cheek as the faint and melodic tinkle of glass wind chimes danced into the silence. Exhausted, she gave in quickly to sleep's persuasive tug, wondering as she did so who had opened the bedroom window . . . knowing as she wondered that no one had.

And then she heard her name. Softly spoken. From a distance. . . . *"Merry."*

Just "Merry," in that deep, raspy brogue she remembered from nights past. It was her dream lover's voice. It sent shivers up her spine and at the same time heated her blood and accelerated the beat of her already pounding heart.

"Where are you?" a voice whispered back. She recognized it as her own, though it seemed to come from far away.

"Here, Merry. Over here. Come quickly. . . ."
Since twilight, she'd listened to the wind pick up as she paced her dark bedroom, Jamie's note clutched in her hand. She'd read and reread his short message: Midnight, the gardener's shed. Jamie.

It was almost midnight now. She couldn't wait any longer to see him.

She slipped silently down the stairs and out the back door. After glancing furtively over her shoulder, she raced across the moonlight-drenched lawn.

No one heard her. No one knew she'd stolen out of her bedroom and into the night.

The chimes Papa had brought home from his last voyage to the Orient tinkled softly. The wind tugged at her nightgown, molding the white cotton to her body, and the cool kiss of midnight dew dampened her slippers as she ran across the grass searching the shadows.

She sensed him before she saw him. Suddenly he was there, tall of build, strong of spirit, with his poet's eyes and his lover's mouth . . . smiling . . . beckoning. Then he had snagged her arm and was dragging her into the dark, into the delicious warmth of his embrace.

His breath was ragged, his hands both rough and caressing as he held her urgently against him. She wound her arms around his neck, loving the scent of heather and sea and desire that clung to his skin.

"Ah, Merry." He feathered a kiss across her brow. "Sweet Merry Clare. It's been so long."

Reckless, hungry, he kissed her, drinking from her mouth with the thirst of a man too long without water.

Breathless, yearning, she opened to him, feeding his hunger, satisfying his thirst with a wantonness that shocked her, with a greed that made her want more of the heaven he promised but never quite delivered. Tonight, she wanted it all.

"*Please,*" she whispered against his parted lips. "*Jamie, I've missed you so. Please, love me now.*"

On a frustrated groan, he lightened his hold, stilled his roaming hands. "*I've missed you, too, girl, and nothing would give me greater pleasure than to love you. No man should be as lucky as me. You are a firebrand. My own little flame. And I want you so bad I hurt with it. But your da would have my hide and blister your pretty backside if I let that happen.*"

"*But I love you, Jamie.*"

"*And I you, lass. But now is not the time. And here, against the side of this old shed, is not the place. Not for a delicate flower like you. You deserve a featherbed and the sanctity of wedding vows to protect your name from scandal.*"

His voice, deep, rich, and lyrical, rumbled like a sea swell against her cheek. "*When then?*" she pleaded, snuggling against the rough wool of his jacket.

He chuckled and hugged her hard. "*Ah, Merry girl, you make it hard on a man's sense of honor.*"

The evidence of how hard pressed against her belly. His maleness was both mystery and enticement to her.

"*Does it hurt bad?*" she asked, all guileless concern as she lowered her hand between them to soothe and explore.

"*Lord, girl.*" He grabbed her hand and dragged it to his lips. "*Have a care.*" He bit her knuckles lightly, then soothed them with a kiss. "*A man can only take so much.*"

"*I hurt too, Jamie.*" Daring as only a young lover could be, she drew his hand to her breast. "*Here.*"

He groaned and cupped her fullness in his palm.

"*And here.*" Inflamed with desire, bold with need, she

lowered his hand to the heat between her thighs. "Make it go away."

With a primal growl, he lowered his head to her breasts, kissing her through the thin nightgown, wetting her straining nipple with his tongue.

It wasn't enough, for either of them. One delicate roll of her shoulder, one deliberate tug of his hand, and her gown dropped to expose her breasts to the cool September midnight and Jamie's marauding tongue.

She arched her back against the weathered shed as he sipped and suckled.

"Do you know how you taste?" he murmured reverently, his hot breath cooling the flesh he'd wet with such exquisite care. "Like the first spring breeze stealing across the highlands to melt the winter snows from the heather."

And then his hand was there, where she needed him most, caressing, stroking, finessing her to a plane of delirium that forced a low, keening sound from deep in her throat.

"And you feel, Lord above, you feel like warm honey, like melting butter. Melt for me Merry girl. Melt for me. . . ."

With a sigh that transformed into a cry of surrender, she did as he asked. His mouth swooped over hers, muffling her love sounds, swallowing her rapturous moan. Pressing her body to the shed with his, he took her to the brink of madness, then caught her in his arms when she toppled over the edge.

Cradling her against him, he brushed the hair from her eyes and rocked her until her trembling subsided. . . .

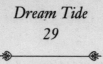

Drenched in perspiration and desire, Merry stretched languidly, matching her breathing to the heavy cadence of her rapidly beating heart.

On one level, she was aware that it was daylight. On another, she clung to sleep, drifting on the lingering scent of sea and heather. The dream was the sweetest one yet. More vivid. More explicit. More everything. And she didn't want it to end. . . .

"Lord, if you aren't tempting."

Her heart quickened with joy. He was still here. Husky with arousal, Jamie's words feathered across her breast as the morning stubble of his jaw whispered across her skin.

Thrilled by the gently abrasive sensation, she threaded her fingers through his hair and drew him closer. With a shivery sigh, she arched into the warmth of his mouth.

His callused hand slid slowly up her thigh. *"Such a temptation for this Irish mother's son,"* he murmured, cupping her bare hip with a lazy, lingering familiarity. Nuzzling, licking, he gave her breast a light, teasing nip, then let go of a sigh that ended as a groan and, with considerable reluctance, rolled away from her.

"No . . . don't go," she heard herself whisper.

"I'm not going anywhere, love."

She opened her sleepy eyes to see him standing in the doorway. Lord, he was beautiful. Long, muscled legs enticingly covered by faded denim. Lean, tan belly. Broad expanse of smooth, sculptured chest sprinkled liberally with crisp black curls.

Thick, sooty lashes framed onyx-black eyes that watched her with a sleepy, sexy smile. She smiled back, nestled deeper into the covers, and closed her eyes . . . until an acute, shocking awareness snapped them open again.

Heart pounding, she stared in horror at the ceiling—then whipped her head back toward the bedroom door, where Patrick Ryan stood watching her.

"Good morning," he said in a deep, melting voice. "Sleep well?"

She stared at him in stunned silence.

"Not a morning person? I'll bet a cut of coffee will set you right. Be right back." He paused, one hand on the door, a patently male grin dimpling his cheeks. "By the way, love . . . I don't know who you were dreaming of, but I sincerely hope it was me."

She closed her eyes and swallowed back a wave of mortification as he headed for the kitchen. Dream about him? Any dream involving Patrick Ryan would have to be a nightmare . . . which this was fast becoming.

Damn the dreams. And damn the man. He'd been watching her. She felt a slow, hot blush spread the length of her body and battled the sensual rush with anger. He called himself a gentleman. She doubted he'd ever been mistaken for one. He was nothing but a rascal and a rogue.

This situation was quickly getting out of hand.

Shaking off the lethargic tug of the dream, she told herself she had to get out of here. Only she wasn't fast enough. She was still calculating the odds of scrambling into her coat and shoes when he sauntered back, a mug of coffee in each hand.

Not about to let him know he was getting to her, she faced him, attempting to train her gaze to stay above belt-buckle level. Not an easy feat, considering he hadn't bothered with a belt, or with the snap on his jeans or, for that matter, with buttoning his fly any farther than half-mast.

He stopped in the threshold and slanted a broad, bare shoulder against the doorjamb. His negligently sexy pose was both unnerving and provocative. Intimately inviting. And entirely too compelling.

She jerked her head back toward the ceiling, wishing she were an ostrich and the bed were the Mojave Desert. In absence of either possibility, she improvised by rolling away from his smiling eyes and yanking the covers over her head.

His soft chuckle drifted over from the doorway. "Come back out and play, Merry," he wheedled, gentle amusement softening his voice.

"Does the word 'eviction' strike any particular chord, Mr. Ryan?"

The mattress shifted with his weight as he eased a hip onto the bed. "You wouldn't do that. Not to a fine Irish lad like me. Besides . . . there's the matter of the lease. I think we're still looking at another ten months."

She pinpointed then exactly what it was that she didn't like about him. He assumed too much. He controlled too much. And if she didn't miss her guess, he did exactly as he damn well pleased, consequences be damned. She knew his kind too well. She'd been married to a man exactly like him.

When that thought settled, she finally understood why he'd struck her as so familiar, and why he had such an unsettling effect on her. Patrick Ryan reminded her of Gavin. Oh, not so much in looks. Though almost as tall as Patrick, Gavin had been slimmer, and his hair was blond. But in attitude, charm, and coaxing ways, the two men could have been brothers.

Like Gavin, Patrick was classically male. Poster-perfect, suitable for framing. Like Gavin, he knew it and took advantage of it. Unfortunately, drawing those parallels made her remember what had drawn her to Gavin in the first place. And it angered her that in spite of recognizing it, she found Patrick Ryan's boldness intriguing.

He tugged playfully on the covers before giving her hip an unauthorized squeeze. "Why don't you drink your coffee, and then you can tell me what's got you so upset."

"I don't recall inviting you in here," she said stiffly.

Patrick smiled unapologetically as she folded back the covers. Even though she was angry and ruffled, her heather-gray eyes still soft with sleep, he was taken again with how pretty she was.

"You're right," he agreed, rising from the bed. "I'll

just leave the coffee on the nightstand and go pour myself a second cup while you get yourself together."

He hadn't even made it to the kitchen when he heard the front door slam. He winced, grinned, and parted the kitchen curtain to get a better look as she hustled across the cobblestone walk toward the big house.

Oh, but she was a fine sight. But madder than a cat who'd lost her catnip. She'd get over it. He'd make sure she did.

Whoa—now there was a definite change of plans. He'd fallen asleep in such a state last night that he'd made a decision upon rising this morning. This little landlord was not for him. He had work to do. A manuscript to draft. A deadline to meet.

Unfortunately, after one look at her soft, sleepy self snuggled in his bed, all his resolve had evaporated like the steam now slowly fading from the windowpanes.

He grinned again when she dropped her keys in her haste, snatched them up angrily, and let herself into the house. His grin faded, however, when he contemplated what he would be letting himself in for if he were to play with the lady's brand of fire, though it had been a nice surprise to find it waiting for him upon his return.

He dropped the curtain. There it was again. That vague and unsummoned thought that it might be nice to have someone waiting. A woman like Merry would definitely be a woman worth coming home to . . .

might even provide a reason to stay home in the first place.

He shrugged off that notion like a dirty shirt. He sensed that Merry was a forever kind of woman. And he knew what happened to men who bought into that. Men like his brother.

Poor Andrew. Deluded into believing himself happy. Rebecca had merely batted her baby blues Andrew's way, and it had been all over for him. Now his life was ruled by routine, midnight feedings, and mortgages.

It wasn't that Patrick didn't approve of Rebecca. In fact, he was rather taken with the the way she devoted herself to Andrew and the kids. It was the restrictions that came with that kind of commitment that he didn't like.

Thinking of Andrew now, recalling that sappy, you-don't-know-what-you're-missing smile he seemed to have perpetually plastered on his face, was enough to renew Patrick's resolve to steer clear of Merry and those promise-me-forever eyes of hers.

Patrick's stomach growled, reminding him he needed more than coffee to start the day.

Food. Now there was a problem he could sink his teeth into. A trip to the market was simple business. Lord, he'd missed being able to have a good hamburger. And a good cold beer.

Not that he couldn't get along without them. He had—for six, long, desert-parched months. They were just another couple of those simple pleasures he'd been looking forward to since he'd helped cap his first oil-well fire with that wild redheaded Texan last March. Since then, he'd eaten as much sand, sweat, and blood, and drunk as much goat milk, as he'd cared to in this life or the next.

For the next few weeks, when he wasn't working on the first draft of his manuscript, kicking back and watching the leaves turn was about as complicated and as dangerous as he wanted the action to get.

And you'll do well to remember that, he chided himself, glancing at the window again. Danger to his mental health and his deadline lurked just behind the walls of the house next door.

"I still can't believe you gave up your apartment for that mausoleum," Cory Baker grumbled around a mouthful of french fries. It was the next day, and Merry and Cory were sharing a quick lunch at the office. "If you ask me, it's just a spooky old relic that'll probably take an oil tanker a year to heat."

Knowing her impulsive decision to buy the house had been out of character, Merry offered her assistant the only explanation she had. "Let's just say I need a change. I saw the ad, took a look, and something told me it was the thing to do. Besides, I got a good buy."

"That's because white elephants usually come with red tags," Cory murmured.

Merry smiled. With her level-headed approach to life and her understated style, Merry was usually the one to caution Cory. Compared to Merry, Cory was as frivolous and fanciful as a balloon bouquet.

Last December, when Merry had conceded that Collectibles, the estate-auction business she'd founded two years ago, had outgrown the format of a one-woman show, Cory Baker had answered her ad for an assistant. When she'd strolled in with her wild tumble of honey-curls, her suede miniskirt, and slogan-of-the-day earrings, Merry had had multiple reservations about hiring her.

During the interview, however, she'd discovered what hadn't met the eye. Behind the "nobody home" image lurked a keen intelligence and a cooperative spirit. What Cory lacked in experience, she made up for in enthusiasm and an uncanny business sense. Though at twenty-four Cory was Merry's junior by eight years, she'd also become a good friend. Friendship notwithstanding, however, Merry's next comment drew from Cory a patently horrified look.

"I've been thinking that if I can get the zoning commission's approval, the house would be an ideal place to move Collectibles. It's a question of finances," Merry explained quickly. "Why pay rent on this office if I don't have to? Think about it. What could be more perfect than running an antique estate business from a Victorian mansion? We could use the downstairs for the business and the second floor for my living quarters."

"And the bats and the bogeymen can take the third floor," Cory groused with a shiver. "That darn place is as creepy as a graveyard. And what about that phantom tenant who goes with the cottage?" she added, still trying to interject reason.

Memories of her encounter with the "phantom tenant" had Merry shifting restlessly in her chair. She'd conveniently forgotten to mention her meeting with Patrick Ryan to Cory. She'd like to forget it herself.

"What about him?" she asked with studied casualness.

"For one thing, you don't know anything about him." Cory snorted. "If he matches the decor around there, he probably comes equipped with a hump on his back and answers to Igor."

Merry pictured Patrick Ryan—sleekly muscled, deeply tanned—and wished that he at least had a wart or two to put a damper on his physical appeal.

"I'm afraid he's part of the deal. He recently signed a year's lease, and honoring it is a condition of the sale. At any rate, his rent will help pay the bills. Besides, I don't anticipate seeing too much of him." She almost choked on the words as she remembered him standing in the bedroom doorway, shirtless, gloriously rumpled, beautifully male. She'd already seen all too much of him. "According to the broker, he isn't around more than two or three months out of the year anyway."

"Oh, yeah . . . he's some sort of a 'free-lance adventurer' or something, right? What the bejesus is a free-lance adventurer, anyway?"

Merry shrugged to cover her discomfort at dissembling. "I don't really know, but I think Max said that last he knew, he was in the Middle East somewhere." If only he were, she added silently.

Cory stared at her long and hard, then shook her head. "You know, I always thought an impulsive streak would look good on you, Mer, but I've got to tell you—you do *not* wear it well."

Merry sighed tiredly. "Cory, listen. For the first time in a long time, something other than my work has me excited. I can't wait to start refurbishing that house. All it really needs is some basic repairs and lots of TLC. And you saw for yourself—it's filled with a treasure trove of antiques."

Merry made her living finding just the right piece for just the right client. Collectibles was only two years old, but she'd learned her trade well during the six years she'd spent assisting a major antique dealer out of Boston. She'd developed an educated eye and knew the moment she'd walked in the mansion's front door that she'd stumbled onto a collector's dream. Why, the Rococo Revival sofa that she'd discovered in the drawing room was, alone, worth a tidy sum. Even with business picking up every month, she hadn't counted on owning pieces like that for many years yet. That's what had made the deal even sweeter.

"So, when are you moving into Dracula's den?" Cory asked, reading Merry's look and capitulating with an "I can't fight it" roll of her eyes.

"As soon as I can sublet my apartment. In the meantime I've already started cleaning it up myself."

"Dusting the cobwebs off the ole tombstones?"

"Will you just stop with the graveyard jokes? Let me enjoy it . . . in fact, *you* might enjoy helping me."

"Not a chance. I don't do windows and I don't do"—reading the warning in Merry's eyes, Cory traded her original analogy for another—"lovely Victorian masterpieces. Besides, I wouldn't deprive you of your great solo adventure for all the bargains at Bloomingdale's. And let's face it, if I'm going to put any effort into anything, it'll be into getting a date for next weekend."

For all her talk, Merry found several excuses over the next few days to avoid returning to the house. Until the furnace was repaired, working there was out of the question anyway. At least that's what she told herself as she lay in bed every night in her apartment. Believing any excuse was easier than admitting she was avoiding Patrick Ryan.

Heat flooded her cheeks whenever she thought of him. And she thought of him far too often. Determined *not* to think about him tonight, she traded one problem for another. She picked up the book from her nightstand and studied it. Bound in rich brown leather, etched in gold, the book of Irish poetry had been softened by time, and—it had struck her when she'd first seen it—by loving hands that had held it.

She'd bought the book a couple of weeks earlier, when, caught in a rainstorm, she'd ducked into a little bookstore. The antique book had caught her eye, and without even opening it, she'd bought it, thinking it would make a nice conversation piece. Not until she'd gotten home had she opened the book, only to receive a shock as she read the inscription inside:

> *To my beloved Merry Clare:*
> *Hold these sonnets close to your heart until I can*
> *hold you close to mine.*
>
> > *Yours, through time,*
> > *Jamie.*
> > *September, 1892*

She was so unnerved that her first impulse had been to return the book. After she'd calmed down, she'd reread the inscription and told herself the unique spelling of her name, the very presence of her name in a hundred-year-old book, was only a rare coincidence. Nothing more.

When her dreams of Jamie and Mary Clare began that night, she rationalized them away also. Obviously they were fostered by the inscription. Maybe such detailed and erotic dreams were unusual for her, but she decided it was just a phase she was going through. Eventually the impact of the eerie coincidence of the Irish woman's name and the sensual dreams would fade as new events in her life took precedence. She knew that if she told Cory about the book and the dreams, the younger woman would begin chattering about supernatural phenomena, the paranormal, and voices from the past. Merry, however, was a believer in facts. And until she either discovered a reasonable explanation for the book and the dreams, or the dreams stopped haunting her sleep, she would tell no one about them.

Merry glanced at her alarm clock and groaned. It was close to midnight. The book, the house, and Patrick Ryan not withstanding, she had a big day tomorrow. She had to get some sleep.

And though she was loath to admit it, she had begun looking forward to the dream. Since the night in Patrick Ryan's bed, it had become more explicit, more sensual, more compelling . . . right down to the last detail and the moment of awakening. It was as if she actually became the other Merry during the night, experiencing her love, living her passion.

She closed her eyes, used to the routine by now. The soft tinkle of glass wind chimes heralded Jamie's arrival as she drifted off to sleep. . . .

The shrill intrusion of Merry's alarm accompanied the dream's climax and wrenched her back to reality. . . .

She forced her eyes open, drew a shaky breath, and glanced at the clock. Six A.M. As she'd come to expect, it had happened again. Another night had passed. Another dream had filled it. And it had ended far too soon.

Touching trembling fingers to her mouth, she yearned for Jamie . . . until she realized she was clutching a piece of paper in her hand.

As her heart did a quick rolling tumble, she flicked on the light and sat up. Even before she unfolded the aged parchment, she had a feeling she knew what she'd find written there: *Midnight, the gardener's shed. Jamie*.

She dropped the note as if it were on fire. Then she threw back the covers and bolted out of bed and into the bathroom. Leaning over the sink, she splashed cold water on her face to clear her head. Of course there was a reasonable explanation. There had to be.

The note must have been tucked between the pages of the book. It must have fallen out—and she'd picked it up in her sleep. Either that or something inexplicable was happening to her. Something she had no control over. Something with implications she didn't begin to understand.

Meeting her own gaze in the mirror, she forced herself to admit to yet another fact . . . one she'd been trying to deny for several days now and could no longer escape.

The poet's eyes and lover's mouth of the wild Irish rogue in her dreams belonged to none other than her adventurous tenant—Patrick Ryan.

THREE

One week later Merry was standing in the center of the mansion's drawing room, listening with half an ear to the mellow buzz of a dozen different conversations floating around her. She stole an appreciative glance around the roomful of people.

A festive fire blazed in the huge, ornate brick-and-tile fireplace. The wall-mounted brass gaslights flickered softly. Overhead, the teardrop-crystal chandelier sparkled with reflected light.

As late as yesterday afternoon, she wouldn't have believed the house would be suitable for habitation, much less entertaining. Cory, however, had had no such reservations. Once she'd accepted the fact that Merry was going through with her plans to move in, Cory had orchestrated this evening's event. A group of twenty or so friends and business associates had gathered, both to satisfy their curiosity and to offer Merry housewarming wishes.

Much as she'd wanted to tackle the cleaning herself, Merry had had to cry uncle. A surge of new business and a sudden opportunity to sublet her apartment had forced her to engage the services of a first-rate cleaning company. She'd offered the electricians and plumbers a bonus if they could complete their work in a week's time. They had done so, with spectacular results.

She'd moved in yesterday and fallen in love with the house all over again. While she couldn't afford to have the whole house done, every room and all the furnishings on the first floor had been restored to their former elegance. The hardwood floors and woodwork gleamed from lemon-scented polish. The patterns in the area carpets, after meticulous and careful shampooing, had come alive with color. The velvet and brocade of the occasional chairs, fainting couches, and love seats had taken on new life.

"Some party, huh?" Cory paused in her nonstop flitting about the room long enough to stuff a canapé delicately into her mouth. "I've got to admit, Mer, now that it's all cleaned up, it really is some house."

"Yes, it's some house. And yes, this is some party. I don't know how you pulled it off."

Cory smiled and shrugged. "Piece o' cake. You look absolutely fabulous in the costume, by the way."

Ah, yes, the costume. Merry glanced at her reflection in the gilt-framed mirror above the mantel and fought the urge to cover herself with the closest drape.

Yards of red satin, bits of white lace, and entirely too much cleavage met her eye. Only for Cory had she consented to wear the dress—and then only because Cory had insisted that the perfect way to show off the house and promote Collectibles' future location was to dress in the style of the period.

Tugging discreetly on the gown's low-cut neckline, Merry decided she looked about as historically authentic as the microwave in the kitchen and as willing as a French courtesan.

"It's a bit much, don't you think? I thought Victorian ladies were known for their sense of propriety, not their lack of it."

"Leave it be." Cory batted Merry's hand away from the low décolletage. "Everyone loves it. As inspirations go, I think it was one of my finest."

"One of your wildest, you mean."

"Speaking of wild, *who* is the gorgeous hunk who just slipped into the room, and *why* is he looking at you like he wants to play lord of the manor to your lusty nimble wench?"

A prickle of awareness, heavily laced with anticipation, eddied down the length of Merry's spine. Very slowly, she looked in the direction of Cory's enthralled gaze. It came as no surprise when the eyes that met hers were Irish-black and glinting with unconcealed interest.

Patrick Ryan raised a glass of wine and one corner of his mouth in greeting. Merry lifted a brow and found new appreciation for the subtleties of a Victorian lady's fan. Fire flooded her cheeks as she fluttered the white lace and whalebone slowly.

"You've been holding out on me, Mer. And I mean big time. *Who* is that man?"

Awareness and anticipation melted to a slow, hot tingling that spread to the tips of her barely concealed breasts before pooling in the pit of her tightening stomach. Fighting irritation with herself for the rush of excitement she felt at seeing him again, Merry smiled tightly. "You might see if he answers to 'Igor.'"

Merry had to give Cory credit. She was managing to keep her chin from hitting the floor—though barely.

"Well, well, well, well, well," Cory drawled, her gaze locked with rapt fascination on Ryan. "So, the adventuring tenant returneth."

And with a purpose, Merry thought uneasily. A sensual challenge burned in the bold gaze that followed every move she made . . . a challenge that suggested he knew her every thought. Lord, she hoped not.

A week ago she'd told herself she never wanted to see Patrick Ryan's cocky, sexy grin again. She'd thought she'd had herself pretty much convinced. The rapid-fire beat of her heart told her otherwise. Loud and clear.

"No sign of a hunchback," Cory mused with undisguised interest. "And with a face like that, I'd even forgive him if he drooled over his supper. So what's the story, Mer?" Cory added suspiciously. "Why didn't you tell me you'd met him?"

She tried for a throwaway shrug. "There's nothing to tell," she lied, then watched in edgy silence as Patrick Ryan pushed away from the wall, wove his way through the crush of people, and cut a path in her direction. "He's back. No doubt he'll soon be leaving again. Listen, I'm going to check on that last batch of crab puffs. Hold down the fort, will you?"

Acting on a strong urge to get away from her tenant, Merry skirted around Cory before she could protest and made a break for the kitchen.

She'd like nothing better than to hate the man. So why didn't she? Because unfortunate and compelling details of their initial meeting kept filtering into her thoughts and wouldn't let her. Like the dark eyes that played and smiled and shimmered with a life all their own. Like the gentle way he'd treated her even when he was teasing her.

Lord, he'd been full of himself. And he enjoyed himself far too much at her expense, she reminded herself as she snatched a mitt from the counter. Latching on to that anger, she turned off the oven. She was bent over, sliding out a baking sheet, when she heard the kitchen door open and close softly behind her.

A slow, thrumming excitement settled deep in her belly, then spread like steam heat through her entire body.

"In most circles," she said, knowing without turning around who had followed her into the room, "party-crashing is still considered impolite."

"I've never claimed to be polite, Merry. And I'm not interested in 'most circles.' What I'm interested in is you."

His voice was as smooth as the fabric of her dress, as rich as deep burgundy wine. And as intoxicating.

She set down the baking sheet with an unsteady hand, damning herself for letting him have this effect on her. Turning to face him, she willed her expression to be as starchy as the lace of her fan.

"What *I'm* interested in, Mr. Ryan, is forgetting I ever met you."

He gave her a slow, sexy smile that relayed what a horrible liar he thought she was.

"Are you? Are you really?"

"Yes." The single word slipped out as barely a whisper and, unfortunately, without a thread of conviction.

"I don't think you want to forget me," he said softly. "And though I've spent the last week or so trying to convince myself that it would be best if I forgot you, I can't. Why is that, do you suppose?"

His voice questioned and challenged and soothed all at the same time. Damn him. And damn those eyes. Besides being as dark and addictive as chocolate, they saw too much. They saw the effect he was having on her.

She swallowed hard, then made a pretense of shrugging off his question as inconsequential. "If you'll excuse me, I've got guests to entertain. *Invited* guests."

"Running away from me again, Merry, love?"

"I am not running away. And I am *not* your Merry love."

"I can't decide," he said, his voice dropping to that

low, melting pitch she'd thought of too often recently, "if I like you better in white or red satin."

Moving another step closer, he reached out and idly fingered the red fabric at her shoulder. Alarmed by the fire his light touch sparked, she jerked away.

He dropped his hand. "I get the feeling you feel threatened by me."

She drew a fortifying breath and immediately regretted it. His devil-black gaze dropped and darkened as he watched her breasts strain above and against the red satin.

"You do not threaten me. You annoy me. Now . . ." Picking up the tray of canapés, she made to slip past him. "Do you mind?"

With a slow, winning grin, he stepped aside. "For now, Merry. But make no mistake," he whispered as she breezed by him and through the door, "we'll finish this later."

By 2:00 A.M. Merry was exhausted from both the party and the tension Ryan had managed to tighten like a harp string inside her. She shooed Cory out the door, insisting she'd done enough and that she could handle the cleanup by herself.

She returned to the drawing room and let her gaze roam slowly about her. The room, now as graceful and opulent as it was intended to be, basked in the glow of a slow-burning fire. Pride filled her. From the moment she'd seen the house, she'd felt a sense of home that had tugged and persuaded and led her to sign on the dotted line. Cory had been right: Buying it had been impulsive. But tonight, seeing the results of what she'd only visualized, she knew she'd done the right thing. She hugged herself as the gaslights cast dancing shadows across the walls, complementing the glow from the fire.

Still, as right as it felt, something was missing. This house—particularly this room—was a natural setting for romance. A yearning both pure and primitive caused a low hollow ache inside her.

It was now a little over two years since the divorce. Her recovery had taken time, but she'd finally realized that Gavin hadn't been worth the tears. But though she was over Gavin, she wasn't over the blow he'd dealt her self-esteem. And she certainly wasn't ready for romance yet.

Undoubtedly it was her strange and fascinating dreams about Jamie and Merry Clare that had left her so restless and dissatisfied. Her curiosity about the young lovers of her dreams was simply piqued. She wanted to know what happened next . . . whether Jamie and Merry Clare ever found happiness together. The dream had not progressed since that night when Merry Clare had so boldly professed her love for Jamie. Every night, the same scene was replayed. And every morning she awakened feeling as hot and needy as the other Merry Clare.

"Your time would be much better spent," she muttered, looking wearily at the party debris around her, "if you'd stick with the business at hand instead of stewing over a stupid dream." Great parties, without exception, came with a price: cleaning up.

It *had* been a great party, she mused, as she slipped off her shoes, except for one thing: her uninvited guest.

After their encounter in the kitchen, he had completely ignored her. Although he didn't appear to be the giving-up kind, he must have done just that. And she found she was unaccountably disappointed.

"You are hopelessly addled," she sputtered as she scooped up a couple of wineglasses. She went into the kitchen to find a tray. As she headed back to the drawing room, she stopped abruptly at the door.

A chilling sense of foreboding swept through her. Her skin tingled and her heart pounded so hard she had to steady herself with a hand on the door frame.

Battling to calm herself, she listened, fearful of the unknown. Nothing. She heard nothing. Just the empty house settling in for the night. Just the eerie wail of a rising wind that skittered around the windows and rattled the glass like an angry ghost shut out of his favorite haunt.

Disgusted by her own histrionics, she reminded herself that she didn't believe in premonitions, or in dreams as prophesies of the future or, in her case, windows to the past. And she wasn't bothered by things that went bump in the night either, she added, drawing a steadying breath.

She pushed through the kitchen door, then froze

once more when her gaze snagged and held on the mirror above the mantel.

Disbelieving, she stared in silence at the reflection that joined hers in the mirror. Standing behind her, meeting her gaze in charged, sensual silence, was her wild Irish rogue, her daring dream lover, Jamie.

Her first thought—when she could form one—was denial. This wasn't real. It couldn't be happening. It was some trick of light and shadows. To prove it, she closed her eyes and counted to ten, confident that when she opened them again, the only eyes staring back at her would be her own.

Slowly, she pried her eyes open. Her confidence and composure splintered like a shattered wineglass when Jamie's soft poet's eyes smiled back at her pale reflection.

The blood in her veins turned to ice; her insides tightened into cold, hard knots. Trapped in a paralyzing fascination, she fought a panic unlike any she'd ever known. It stalled her breath and weakened her knees. Her heart caught, then slammed into a hard, ragged cadence.

She watched, electrified, as Jamie's reflection glided near . . . so near, she swore she felt the warmth of his breath fan her shoulder. She had no choice but to return his dark-eyed stare, aware as she did of every charged molecule of air surrounding her, every faintly drawn breath in the suddenly suffocating room.

"I've decided I know what our problem is."

Her heart went crazy at the sound of his raspy Irish brogue. Strong fingers gripped her arm. She let him turn her slowly toward him as the tray in her hand landed with a soft thud on the carpet by her feet. An all-consuming fear constricted her vocal cords and captured the scream erupting inside.

He held both shoulders lightly. "Merry—what is it, love? You look like you've seen a ghost."

The hauntingly gentle eyes that watched her narrowed in concern. It was that concern, the solid strength of his warm hands on her arms, and the way he spoke her name that finally penetrated her terror.

Rational thought seeped slowly into her consciousness. With it came a profound sense of relief.

She slumped weakly against him, pressing her forehead to his chest. "Oh, God, Patrick," she whispered, latent fear threading a breathless quality through her voice. "It's you."

"Well, of course it's me, love." His hands tightened on her shoulders as he searched her face. "Are you all right?"

"Aside from having the life scared out of me, I'm fine." You couldn't have proven it from her heart. It still pounded wildly, but from outrage now instead of fear.

"What the devil are you doing here?" she snapped, pulling herself together and putting some distance between them. She must be more exhausted than she thought, conjuring up ghostly lovers. Meanwhile a flesh-and-blood rake was giving her all the earthly problems she could handle. "And how did you get in?"

He smiled, his gaze straying to her breasts, which gave away her agitation with their heavy rise and fall.

"I never left," he said, his attention returning to her face. "It's a big house, love. There are many corners to explore when a man is waiting to get a lady alone. Don't look so surprised. I told you we'd finish later."

She pressed a hand to her temple. Would the man never stop?

"Now I know it's late," he said, moving toward her. "And by the look in your pretty heather eyes, I can see how tired you are. But the truth is, love, that I haven't been able to quit thinking about you. In spite of the fact that I've tried to argue myself out of seeing you more times than I care to count."

Overwhelmed, Merry stared at him in silence.

"So, I've decided that there's nothing for it but to have my say . . . and I intend for you to listen." He paused as if waiting for her to challenge him. When she didn't, he continued, "Fate seems to have had a hand in our meeting. I'm not sure yet why, I only know I can't let it go. Not yet. Not until I get the chance to know you better. Not until you get to know me."

She managed to raise a brow. His comments should have sounded arrogant, but instead his fatalistic tone was strangely compelling.

"Once you do get to know me, it'll be your call whether to pursue the relationship or not."

He gave her a moment to absorb his meaning. Then he advanced slowly toward her.

Compelled by forces she did not even begin to understand, she met his gaze in the firelight.

"You're tired," he said soothingly as he pulled her slowly, effortlessly, into his arms. "Your resistance is low. Here's fair warning, love. . . ." He touched a hand to her hair. "I intend to take advantage."

His black eyes strayed to her mouth and lingered. "You have the most incredible mouth. I've spent too many nights wondering what it would taste like." Spreading his fingers wide across her throat, he tipped her face to his with a gentle pressure of his thumb under her chin.

Without further hesitation, without even a hint of apology or a pretense of request, he bent to her, slanting his mouth over hers.

In spite of his warning, she was taken by surprise, and she opened her mouth to object. Choosing to interpret her protest as an invitation, he deepened the kiss, claiming her mouth with his tongue.

Boldly, greedily, he bent over her. Defiantly, angrily, she arched against him. He responded by tightening his hold, compelling her surrender with the sheer magnetism of his physical sensuality, daring her to resist.

Though she knew she should fight him, she was caught up in the storm he had created. All too susceptible to the need she felt in him and the answering need she felt within herself, she succumbed to the skill of his kiss, the magic of his caress, the achingly poignant sense that this was familiar and right.

The fists she'd knotted against his chest relaxed and clutched weakly at his shirt. Then her arms rose to wind recklessly around his neck. And then, it seemed, there was nothing on heaven or earth that could have stopped him. He groaned his approval, and the seduction began in earnest.

He romanced her body with his own, encouraging her response with the insistent pressure of his hips, demanding her submission with the heated brush of his hands across her back.

Without breaking the kiss, he scooped her into his arms and settled, with her on his lap, onto the closest love seat.

"You are incredible," he whispered, lifting his head long enough to look into her eyes.

"I am insane," she managed between deep, ragged breaths.

He smiled as he stroked the corner of her mouth with an unsteady but gentle thumb. He kissed her again, this time tenderly.

"Incredible," he repeated, looking and sounding as shaken as she felt.

"Incredibly insane, then," she conceded, fighting to deny the mindless desire he'd kindled.

He chuckled. The sound was warm and rich and wrapped around her senses like a soft, seductive caress. She knew she should be trying to get away from him but told herself he wouldn't let her go anyway. The sad truth was that she wanted to stay. She was terrified by the need he evoked in her, by the lavish sensations she'd experienced during his kisses, by the wild desire to experience more.

His eyes glinted with passion.

She met them beseechingly. "What are you doing to me?"

He expelled a shaky breath. "The question, love, is what are *you* doing to *me*?"

"Me? I didn't invite this. And why am I letting it happen?" This she asked more of herself than of him. "I don't even know you."

The oddest look came over his face.

"You know me," he said at last with a curious softness that confused her even more. "And you want to know me better."

Damning those eyes again for seeing so much more than she wanted him to see, she shook her head. "I don't even know myself when I'm around you. This isn't me. Nothing about this is real."

He smiled gently and lowered his mouth again. When he raised his head, she felt dazed, yearning. Each pulse point in her body begged to be stroked . . . the way Jamie stroked Merry Clare in her dreams.

"Tell me that wasn't real," he whispered, scattering slow, random kisses across her face. "Convince me you didn't want it. That you don't want me to do it again."

With every word, every caress, she became more deeply mired in the maelstrom of sensual pleasure he created. It was as if he *did* know her . . . her every want, her secret needs.

Lowering his mouth to the curve of her shoulder, he nipped her lightly. She shivered, arched, and made a restless, needy little sound in her throat. It was all the invitation he required. His hand stole up and covered her breast. Her nipple hardened, responding instinctively to a lover's touch.

"Ah, Merry. You are so responsive. A firebrand. My own little flame."

His words—*Jamie's words*—cut through the sensual haze like a buzz saw. She shot off his lap and backed several shaky steps away . . . away from his drugging kisses and consuming caresses. Away from the words that came directly from her dreams and made it impossible to separate fantasy from reality.

"Who *are* you?" she demanded, fighting to control the panic in her voice. "Why are you doing this to me?"

His eyes glittered darkly. "I wasn't aware that I was doing anything to you. With you, yes. For you, definitely. Come back, Merry. We'll do much much more."

She shook her head, almost dizzy with the mix of reality and midnight dreams.

"Am I really so frightening?" he asked with a puzzled frown.

"Yes," she answered without thinking. "No," she recanted quickly, but too late to undo the damage. "I don't know," she admitted finally. "You . . . you overwhelm me."

"I make you feel things."

Her silence confirmed his conclusion.

"And want things."

She hugged her arms around her waist and looked away from the truth of his words. She had to think. To do that, she had to get away from him.

"What I want is for you to leave. Now," she insisted with a determination she didn't really feel.

He considered her for a few seconds. She could see that he sensed the power he had over her. That if he chose, he could take her in his arms again and with little more than a few heated kisses have her willing and writhing against him. And as they faced each other with nothing but the dying fire as witness, she questioned why she was bothering to fight it.

"You're right," he said, surprising her. "This is happening too fast." His voice, like his words, was very gentle. "You're tired. I took advantage. But then, I warned you I would."

She didn't know if it was relief or regret that rushed through her body. "And you're a man who always makes good on his threats?"

"Always," he assured her.

"And do you honor your promises as well?" she asked, prompted by pure instinct to challenge him with his own words.

His eyes narrowed, then crinkled at the edges in a

self-mocking smile. "I did make you a promise, didn't I?"

"You promised the next call would be mine."

He was silent for a moment, as if he was considering taking it back. Finally, he shrugged.

"And isn't it a shame you have such a good memory, Merry." The carefree Irish rogue was back. "We're all entitled to a weak moment. Your vulnerability prompted one of mine. I hope I won't live to regret it."

Finding strength in this small victory, she straightened her shoulders and lifted her chin. Suddenly, it seemed very important that she convince him—and herself—that she would not be manipulated.

"I'm neither vulnerable nor malleable, Patrick."

He studied her thoughtfully. "No, I can see that you're not. What are you then, Merry? And the big question—what are you going to be to me?" His eyes, full of promises and passion, dared her to pretend she didn't recognize the chemistry between them.

She recognized it, all right. It was fierce and demanding and it frightened her far more than when she'd thought she was facing her dream lover come to life.

"The only thing I'm going to be to you is your landlord," she insisted, knowing she had to get away from him before she lost what ground she had gained. "Nothing more. And not even that, if you insist on playing this little game you so obviously enjoy playing."

Walking boldly past him, she swept aside her long skirts and strode directly to the front door.

After a moment he followed her.

She willed herself to stand silent and staunch, to stare at the oak floor. She could feel his intense gaze on the top of her head as he stopped in front of her. His unique, rugged scent tickled her senses when he leaned closer.

"One thing you should know up front, Merry. I don't play games."

Ever so gently, he cupped her shoulders in his large hands and placed a kiss on her forehead. "Call if you need me. For anything."

Putting up a shield of anger to hide the unwanted need she felt for him, she said, "When hell freezes over."

He laughed softly, gave her shoulders a quick, possessive squeeze, then left.

FOUR

Hell froze over approximately twenty-four hours later. At any rate it did in Merry's little corner of the world.

She'd managed to avoid her bothersome tenant all day Saturday, the day after the party. At least physically. Thoughts of him, however, stuck with her like a common cold. Not that there was anything common about Patrick Ryan.

His image was always there. Smiling. Teasing. Taking. Tickling her senses the way a cough tickles the throat and won't let a body forget she's sick.

When she went to bed that night, exhausted, she didn't even look at the book of poetry on her bedside table. But thoughts about the book, like thoughts about her tenant, kept her awake well into the night. When she finally drifted off, both the book and the man affected her sleeping thoughts as well.

As usual, it was in the deepest part of the night that the dream began again, this time with a new twist. . . .

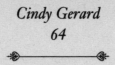

With nothing but the moon, the heather, and the chill of night as witness, Merry leaned heavily against Jamie. Her heart pounded wildly in the aftermath of his exquisite loving; her body trembled in remembrance of her first delicious taste of fulfillment.

Jamie's tenderness, his skillful mouth and knowing fingers, had brought her a pleasure that was both frightening and thrilling in its magnitude.

"I love you Jamie."

"Aye," he whispered back, his breathing as labored and shallow as hers. "And I love you."

"But you're still hurting. I want to . . . to make it better."

He hugged her fiercely and pressed a kiss to the top of her head. "It doesn't matter, lass. I can wait. And it will all be worth it."

She sensed then what he was about to tell her. Why he had wanted to meet her here at midnight by the old gardener's shed. Dread shoved aside latent passion. "You'll be leaving, then?"

Easing down to the cushion of grass, he leaned back against the shed and drew her onto his lap. Tucking her feet inside the folds of his jacket, he wrapped her in his arms.

"There's no other way."

"We could talk to Papa," she suggested earnestly.

"And have him throw me out on my arse and lock you in your room until you're old and gray? He won't have it, Merry. Your da will not be havin' his only daughter lower

herself to marry a stable hand. I must go to America. It's the only way. I'll make my fortune and make you proud. He won't be able to deny me then."

"But it's so far," she cried, trying to keep the desperation from her voice. "And it could take years."

"Nay, girl. They say the streets in America are paved with gold. A man who's not afraid to work can make his fortune in no time. That's what I'll be about. And then I'll send for you."

"What if he won't let me go?"

"I'll come and get you. In my fancy britches and with my pockets full of gentlemen's gold, I'll show him I deserve his respect."

"When?" she whispered so softly he could hardly hear. "When will you go?"

He drew a shuddering breath and held her to his heart. "My ship sails within the hour."

She pulled away from him. "So . . . so soon?"

"Aye," he said, meeting the heartbreak in her eyes.

"I'll wait for you." Her voice broke, but she was determined to be strong for him. "You won't forget me?"

He crushed her against him. "I'd sooner forget my name, my Irish heritage. On my mother's grave, Merry, I'll think of you morning and night. I'll remember the sweetness of your mouth, the gentle warmth of your heather-gray eyes, the fire in your heart, and the love in your soul." Gripping her shoulders, he forced her to look at him. "So no tears, darlin'. You'll not be rid of me as easy as you're thinking."

Digging into the pack he'd dropped beside them, he drew

out a package and pressed it into her hands. "Keep this with you always, and we'll never truly be apart."

With trembling fingers she unwrapped the parcel.

"Jamie, it's beautiful," she said, drawing out the lovely leather-bound volume of poetry.

"Open it," he urged softly.

A tear fell unchecked when she read the inscription.

"Oh, Jamie—"

"I must go, Merry."

She bit back a cry. "Kiss me, Jamie. Kiss me like the first time."

He smiled gently and tipped her face to his. "To first times, Merry. We'll have many. Just you wait and see."

She clung to him, her bravery giving way to grief. "What will I do without you?"

"You'll make plans," he said with false brightness. "You'll figure out how you want to fill the great, grand house I'll be building for you. I'll write you, Merry. I'll send the letters to my cousin, Sean. He'll see that you get them. Will you write to me, lass?"

"Every day."

He smiled at that and looked down at the book of sonnets clutched in her hand. "You'll have the book to remember me."

"Oh, Jamie, I must give you something, too." She touched an unsteady hand to her throat and the gold chain that held her mother's locket. Without hesitation, she slipped it over her head and placed it over his.

He clutched the locket, still warm from her body, in his

hand. "*I can't take this. It was your ma's. It's all you have left of her—*"

She pressed her fingers to his lips, silencing him. "*You must. It's the closest I can come to giving you my heart.*"

A rustling in the bushes brought her head up. Her gaze flew to his.

"*That'll be Sean,*" *he said soberly.* "*He'll be anxious to get on the road and to the wharves. I'm out of time, love.*"

She threw herself into his arms.

He touched a hand to her cheek, brushing away her tears. "*Soon, Merry. We'll be together again soon.*" *Then he rose and pulled her with him. After a final longing look, he set her away.*

She clutched his gift to her breast. Tears clouded her vision as she watched him turn and disappear into the night. "*Go with God, Jamie. Go with God. . . .*"

It was a long way to daylight when Merry awoke. She was crying, and she was cold. The strength of the dream and the love Merry Clare felt for Jamie had shaken her badly. Such sadness. Such passion.

Not quite fully awake but conscious enough to grasp the fact that it had only been a dream, she still felt the pain of Merry and Jamie's parting. She hugged the book of poetry to her breast, only then realizing she held it, and that what she held seemed to be the very book that Jamie had given Merry Clare all those years ago.

She felt as if she were losing her grip on reality.

Were her dreams the product of her overactive subconscious? Or were her dreams showing her what had actually happened in the past?

She stared at the book with troubled eyes. She thought of Patrick Ryan—the embodiment of Jamie—and for the hundredth time tried to explain away the parallels. But how could she explain them when she couldn't even explain the dreams?

Maybe she was going crazy—stark raving mad. What other possible answer could there be?

As she lay there struggling for an answer, she became slowly aware that the dreams were not her most pressing problem. Her bedroom was as frigid as—oh, Lord, was she really going to think it? It was as frigid as a tomb.

Suddenly she heard a distant pounding . . . no, it was more like a rapping. The sound sent a shiver down her spine. A shiver of fear.

She bolted straight up in bed, all her senses on overload.

Rap . . . rap, rap . . . RAP!

With passages of Edgar Allan Poe's haunting poetry ringing in her mind, she clutched her blankets around her and listened, trying to identify the source of the noise. It sounded like someone—or something—was hammering from somewhere deep in the bowels of the house.

Shivering with both cold and apprehension, she forced herself out from beneath her covers. She grabbed her robe from the foot of the bed and shrugged into it. As she tightened the belt and plunged her feet into her slippers, she cocked an ear toward the hallway and listened.

Rap . . . rap, rap, rap . . . RAP !!!

If it was a burglar, it was an incompetent burglar, she reasoned, as she tiptoed to the bedroom door. Or anyway, one who didn't believe in sneak attacks. The hammering had grown loud enough to wake the dead.

Oops, there she went again. She shuddered and tried unsuccessfully not to remember Cory's description of the house. *Cold as a tomb. Spookier than a graveyard at midnight. Mausoleum.*

"Damn Cory and her graveyard humor," she muttered.

At that point she found herself hoping it *was* only a burglar. At least then she'd know what she was dealing with.

She stepped quietly out into the hall. The oak floors felt like ice beneath her slippered feet. The old house was full of shadows and drafts, and now, those teeth-rattling bumps in the night too.

"There is a logical explanation for this," she chanted through chattering teeth. Yet the darkness intensified her isolation. The cold magnified the sounds. She jumped when another loud, rhythmic banging rattled the windows.

Clutching her robe tighter around her throat, she inched down the stairs and groaned when she realized she was reciting "Now I lay me down to sleep" under her breath to the cadence of "Quoth the Raven, 'Nevermore.'"

"Get a grip," she ordered herself as her foot reached the bottom step. She drew a steadying breath, her hand clutching the newel post. Try as she might, though, she couldn't shake the chilling premonition that something awful was about to happen. And as she stood in the dark, wondering whether to call the police or work up the nerve to check out the basement, something awful did happen.

The whole house started to groan and vibrate like a volcano on the verge of eruption. The pounding escalated to a rapid succession of booming, brittle, teeth-jarring clanks.

She quit thinking. She just reacted. She abandoned ship.

She raced for the kitchen door, threw it open, and half ran, half stumbled down the porch steps. With the wind nipping at her heels, she flew across the cobblestone walk and attacked Patrick Ryan's door with both fists.

She pounded for what seemed like hours before she heard a muffled "I'm coming . . . I'm coming" from the other side of the door. "What, in the name of all that's holy—"

His unfinished question dangled in the frostbitten air when he threw open the door and Merry tumbled into his arms.

She couldn't imagine what he must think. She really didn't care. The fact that she was quivering like a flagpole in a big wind, her eyes wild, her hair even wilder, didn't even cross her mind.

All she could think about was the strength of the arms steadying her, the heat radiating from the bare chest pressed against her cheek.

"Merry." The concern threaded through his sleep-graveled voice made it even deeper. Gripping her arm, he pulled her inside and out of the chill. "What is it, love? What's the matter?"

She couldn't speak, her teeth were chattering so hard.

"Come, sit down. Tell me what's wrong."

He drew her with him into the living room. Peripherally aware that he was barely zipped into hurriedly tugged-on jeans and nothing else, she let him settle her onto the sofa.

With his hands in her hair, soothing her, she finally managed, in fragmented bits and pieces, to tell him about the cold house, the hammering in the basement, and finally the groaning vibrations.

"You sit tight," he said, squeezing her shoulders to punctuate his order. "You're not to go anywhere, do you hear me? I'll check things out and be right back."

He grabbed a beat-up leather jacket from the coat tree by the door and shrugged into it, then shoved his bare feet into a pair of worn loafers.

"Patrick!" she blurted out as he headed outside.

With one hand on the door he looked back over his shoulder.

"Be careful."

He grinned engagingly. "You forget, love. I'm Irish. And as the saying goes: If you're lucky enough to be Irish, you're lucky enough. Don't worry, Merry. I'll be fine." Then he winked and headed across the cobblestones in a purposeful lope.

The next thirty minutes were the longest in her life. What if something happened to him? What if it *was* a prowler, and he had a gun? She should have insisted that he call the police. If he got hurt—or worse—she'd never forgive herself. In fact her sense of loss would be devastating if—No. She would not allow herself to think the worst. She traded that thought for another consideration. What if it was nothing? What if she'd "dreamed" the entire episode, just as she'd dreamed about Merry and Jamie? No noise, no cold house, no pounding. What if she *was* going crazy?

She was so engrossed in her thoughts that she didn't hear Patrick open the door. He caught her anxiously pacing the living room. She started toward him, then checked herself and the look of relief on her face when she saw his measuring grin.

"Surely that's not concern etched on your pretty brow? No?" He didn't look the least put out as he hung up his jacket and turned back to her. "Well, you've got to admit it. Against all odds, it would seem there's frost on the pumpkins in hell this morning."

Had he sounded smug, or arrogant, or even victorious over the fact that she was having to eat the words she'd uttered only hours ago, she would have been angry. But he was none of the above.

What he was, was handsome, sexy, protective, and

extremely likable standing there in his faded jeans with his bare feet shoved into those ratty loafers.

She really had no choice. It was past time she showed a little grace around him. And his grin was positively infectious. She returned it with a shaky one of her own.

"I see I'm not the only one with a good memory. I truly hope I don't end up regretting everything I say to you."

He smiled and moved toward her. "Say yes now, Merry, and I promise—neither of us will regret it."

The air crackled with sensual heat as their gazes collided. Lord, he was a temptation. All that dark, touchable hair, those black, flashing eyes, that broad, muscled chest. And though he could have easily moved in for the kill, he stopped a mere breath away, leaving her a choice, just as he'd promised. Not that he didn't wheedle a little.

"Come on—take a chance."

For a moment the urge to succumb overpowered her. Then rationality returned, and with it the realization that for the second time in as many weeks, she was once again dressed in her nightshirt facing a man she barely knew.

"What . . . what's going on over there?" she asked, casting a worried look toward the big house. She wrapped her robe more tightly around her.

"Oh, that." He smiled again, this time in reassurance. "It's all taken care of. What you were experiencing was the untimely fussing of a cranky old furnace."

First relief, then a profound sense of embarrassment, flooded her. "The furnace?"

"No goblins, love," he said, exercising his uncanny ability to see her thoughts behind her eyes, "although there was certainly enough rattling to shake the dust off a skeleton or two. You must have been scared senseless."

His fitting analogy made her feel less foolish . . . but only marginally.

"Is it going to blow up?"

"No. It was just complaining a bit. The problem was easily solved, and now it's working fine. In an hour or so your house will be as toasty warm as a roasted marshmallow."

"The plumbers were supposed to have fixed it."

"There's nothing mechanically wrong with the furnace, Merry. Come into the kitchen. I'll put on some coffee and give you a thumbnail account of the workings of hot-water heat."

With patience and precision he did just that, explaining air locks and trapped steam and how to bleed radiators of compressed air so the pipes don't rattle like a chain gang making their great escape. And all the while he fed her information, he also plied her with coffee and cream cheese and bagels. Topped off with his irrepressible Irish charm.

As she sat there at his kitchen table in her nightshirt and robe, facing him in his faded old jeans, she became acquainted with a Patrick Ryan she hadn't expected to meet. A man she liked very much. Perhaps too much.

By the time the sun decided to put in an appearance, he had her smiling and, to his obvious delight, even laughing at his outrageous accounts of his recent adventures in Saudi Arabia. As unlikely as it seemed, she began wondering how she could ever have found him threatening. In fact, she wanted to know a lot more about him.

In the next moment, however, she was reminded of exactly what kind of threat he presented . . . and that she couldn't afford the luxury of getting to know him better.

He had stopped talking and reached across the table to pour her more coffee. She watched the play of muscles over his bare shoulders, the smooth expanse of deeply tanned skin, the assurance with which he moved. She looked up, and their eyes locked. His were dark with invitation, and, she was sure, with awareness of her thoughts.

He was heart-stoppingly gorgeous, had a witty intelligence, and had proven to be kind and amiable. This was a man she could easily fall in love with. As shocking and frightening as that thought was, it was also the boost she needed to make herself pull back before she got any closer.

Patrick Ryan was TROUBLE with capital letters. Heartbreak with an Irish brogue. And he was the last kind of hassle she needed in her life again. Gavin had been just like that. All flash and fun and savvy. He'd swept her off her feet, into his bed, and into a marriage she'd thought made in heaven. But, heaven had turned to hell and she hadn't been the same since. She thought he loved her. It turned out she was just a convenience, and when she was no longer convenient, he'd packed his bags and walked away. On to bigger things. More adventurous things. No hard feelings, right, Merry?

She shivered, remembering how casually he'd thrown away seven years of marriage. She'd understood then that men like Gavin—men like Patrick Ryan—approached life with exactly the same attitude: What can I take from it? Gavin had taken and she had given—gladly, blindly, until the day he'd left. Now she wasn't sure if she had anything left to give another man. She was sure only that she would never put herself in a position where she could be hurt or used like that again.

And she had to get out of this particular man's kitchen before he charmed her into thinking she had another round left in her.

She looked quickly down into her empty coffee cup. "Well, I think I've imposed on you long enough."

When she looked up, he was studying her thoughtfully. "No imposition. And I'd really like for you to stay a bit longer."

She shook her head, rose to her feet, and stood stiffly, her pose a silent communication that this was as far as she was willing to go.

"Thank you, but no. I've got a hundred things to do today. I'm sure you do too. Again, thanks—for everything. And I'm really sorry I interrupted your sleep." She shrugged apologetically.

"Then you've got a lot to be sorry for."

Her questioning frown compelled him to explain.

"I haven't had a good night's sleep since I laid eyes on you, love."

He smiled at her self-conscious silence, a lazy, knowing smile that suggested he knew she wasn't sleeping well either.

"Would you like me to come with you to make sure everything's still working all right then?" he asked, diffusing the tension.

"No," she said quickly. Too quickly. Realizing that, she forced herself to slow down. "No. Thank you. I'm sure it will be fine. If not, I'll call the plumber. I've taken enough of your time."

"My time is yours, Merry." His eyes both invited and challenged. "Anytime."

"Yes, well, I'd better go." With that, she backed toward the door and let herself out.

She forced herself to walk slowly across the cobblestone walk. Her heart, however, beat anything but slowly as she wondered if she'd just escaped the worst chapter in her life, or if she'd run away from the best.

"You're holding out on me again, aren't you?"

It was Monday morning, and Cory had been watching Merry like a dog waiting for a discarded bone. Merry glanced up from the inventory sheets of the Cambridge estate and tried to look relaxed. "Holding out?"

Cory twisted her lips into an impatient little pucker.

She tucked her pencil into the wealth of her thick French braid and leaned forward, her pose encouraging confidence. "Come on, Mer. Fess up. Did something happen after the party that I should know about?"

Merry returned her attention to the inventory. "Party?" she asked absently.

"Is there an echo in here?" Frustrated, Cory flattened her palms on her desk. "You know what I'm talking about. Something happened, didn't it? Something that one minute makes you look dreamy-eyed, rosy-cheeked, and mellow, and the next makes you as edgy as a steak knife. You're distracted to the point of misfiling—yes you did, you misfiled the Talbot account," Cory insisted, cutting off Merry's denial. "And you look as if the last thing you did in your bed last night was sleep. Now I'll ask you again, real nice: What happened after I left? This has something to do with Igor the Adventurer, doesn't it?"

Merry shifted uneasily in her chair. Memories shuttled forward in harried disarray, starting with the morning she'd awakened in Patrick Ryan's bed. A liquid heat shimmered through her body as she thought of it, and of his kisses the night of the party, of his promise that he wasn't playing games. Of the gentle way he'd treated her yesterday when she'd stormed into his arms like a schizophrenic rambling about vibrating houses and Edgar Allan Poe.

She looked up and met Cory's probing frown.

"I . . . I've just had a few nights of restless sleep, that's all," she hedged.

Cory eyed her suspiciously. "Zo . . . you're not zleeping vell?" she asked in her best Freud imitation.

Merry sighed. A long, deep, giveaway sigh that was out before she could stop it.

"Something isn't right, Mer. And you know what? Something hasn't *been* right since you decided to buy that house."

"The house is not the problem."

"Aha!" Cory pounced on the show of surrender. "So you admit there is a problem." She bounced up, snagged the coffeepot, and filled their cups. "Tell Mama all about it."

Merry leaned back in exasperation, deciding she could learn to hate Mondays. She looked at Cory, shook her head, and gave it up. It was just a question of time before Cory broke down her resistance, anyway.

Besides, maybe she did need to talk to someone—at least about the dream—or the little men with the butterfly nets and the white suits were going to come and cart her off to a place where she could weave baskets all day.

"You'll think I've gone off the deep end."

"Old 'She's a Brick' Thomas? Never. Now what's up? Confess. D'you tear the tag off a mattress, or jaywalk, or what? Whoops." Cory grimaced when she saw the look in Merry's eyes. "I guess whatever it is isn't so funny, huh?"

"It should be funny, but it isn't."

Concerned, Cory sat back. "Let's hear it."

She drew a deep breath. "You know that little bookstore on Fifth?" When Cory nodded, she continued, telling her about how she had come to buy the book.

Cory set her coffee mug down expectantly. "Annnddddd . . ."

Merry opened the bottom desk drawer and pulled out her purse. Inside the purse was the book. She removed it and, after debating a moment, offered it to Cory.

"Nice," commented Cory, handling the fragile volume with the respect it deserved.

"Open it."

Cory's gaze brightened with unasked questions as she opened the book and read the hundred-year-old inscription. Eyes wide, she glanced at Merry, then read it again.

"Oh my. Oh. My. Merry . . ." Her eyes were wide, her voice breathless. "This is made out to you. I mean, it's not *Mary* with an *a*, but *Merry* with an *e* and an extra *r*. It even has your middle name." Cory looked up and swallowed hard. "Holy Twilight Zone, Batgirl. This is like, totally weird."

Merry smiled tightly. "Not exactly the way I would have put it, but I believe you summed it up nicely." She rose from her chair, tugged her suit jacket into place, and paced to the window. "There's more. Ever since I bought the book, I've been having these . . . these dreams." Crossing her arms over her breasts, she glanced nervously over her shoulder to meet Cory's captivated gaze.

"What kind of dreams?"

"The kind that, in your words, make me look dreamy-eyed, rosy-cheeked, and like the last thing I did in my bed last night was sleep."

Cory glanced at the inscription again. "About . . . Jamie?"

Merry felt her cheeks redden. "Yes."

"Oh, wow. Is he . . . I mean . . . what does he look like?"

This was the hard part. She hesitated, then blurted it out. "Try Igor on for size."

If possible, Cory's eyes grew even wider. "Patrick Ryan? He looks like Patrick Ryan? Oh wow. Oh. Wow. This is just incredible. You have these dreams about this gorgeous hunk, and then suddenly, out of the blue, he appears in the flesh. This is *weird*, Merry. I mean *reeeally* weird."

"Holy Stephen King, Robin," Merry mimicked sarcastically, "I thought we'd already established that."

"What we *haven't* established is what it all means."

Merry realized that she wasn't prepared to speculate on the idea of unknown forces at work. Neither was she prepared to tell Cory the extent of her encounters with Patrick Ryan.

"What it means," she said firmly, "is that I've been putting in long hours, I'm frustrated with the Calhoun account, and maybe I need some time off."

"Yes to all of the above," Cory agreed. "But it

doesn't explain the inscription. Or the fact that Patrick Ryan is the image of Jamie." Cory tapped her index finger thoughtfully on her lower lip. "Can you say 'paranormal,' boys and girls?"

Merry suppressed a shudder. "I don't buy into that stuff. I can't explain it either, but bottom line, it's just a wild coincidence."

"If you say so." Cory's tone was clearly patronizing. "Just like it's a coincidence that you decided on 'impulse' to buy that spooky old house. That is so unlike you, Merry. For as long as I've known you, you've been a chrome, smoked-glass, and track-lighting kind of girl. You've always said that's what made it so easy for you to deal in antiques—you never got attached to them."

"Maybe years of dealing with all that opulence has finally rubbed off on me."

"Yeah, right. Sorry, but you can't convince me that someone, or some*thing*, didn't pull some strings on that deal."

Merry didn't want to hear about the paranormal or anything else in that line. If she couldn't come up with a logical explanation, she didn't want to hear one at all.

She sighed, avoided Cory's thoughtful frown, and tried to put it all out of her mind. When the phone rang, bringing the promise of another lucrative account, she managed to do just that—at least for the rest of the day.

FIVE

As he packed steaks, salad makings, and a bottle of wine into a picnic basket, Patrick questioned again why he was going to such lengths to win over his pretty landlord. True, he'd always been a man who went after what he wanted. But if the lady wasn't willing, he stopped right there. It was 'so long, keep in touch, have a good life.' No problem.

So, what's the problem here, Ryan? he asked himself as he watched Merry pull into her drive Friday evening, a full five days after she'd pounded on his door at 4:00 A.M.

The problem was, he'd finally seen her smile that morning they'd shared coffee and bagels in his kitchen. The problem was that when she'd smiled, he realized how anxious he'd been to see it. The effect it had had on him had been utterly unanticipated—sort of like a singeing flame, a melting heat, and a mellow awakening all at the same time.

It was damn irritating, this preoccupation he had with her, his inability to get his feelings under wraps. He'd told himself that once he kissed her, his curiosity would be satisfied and he could be on his way. After all, wasn't she the kind of woman he'd always made it a practice to steer clear of? A woman who could make even a wanderer like him think of putting down roots?

Besides, she'd done the equivalent of saying no. That ought to have been the end of it. It might have been—if not for the contradictory message he'd seen in her eyes. Those beautiful heather eyes of hers had gone liquid whenever she'd let herself look at him. Those eyes spoke for her. And what they said was a resounding and unqualified yes.

He admired the way she tried to fight it. Admired her independence too. Yet when she had needed help, she'd instinctively come to him. That said something, too, didn't it? She'd trusted him. She had actually let her guard down for a while that morning as they'd talked. But then, as abruptly as she'd awakened him from sleep, she'd closed herself off again. Closed the door, locked it, and latched it.

Frankly, it had nettled. That inviting glimpse into her vulnerable side had whetted his appetite to know even more about Merry Thomas.

What it all meant, he didn't know. Covering the basket with a checkered cloth, he headed out the door intending to find out—even though he was wading into murky water and not at all sure of the depth. Even though he knew he should take his cues from her and back off before he got in any deeper. Funny thing, though: He suddenly wanted to go deeper . . . much deeper. . . .

Whistling a jaunty Irish tune, he headed across the cobblestone walk, ready to accept anything but a no. Ready to admit to anything but this gnawing suspicion that he just might be looking for some permanency in his life . . . and that Merry Thomas might meet that need.

"Hi," he said when she opened the back door, all bright, surprised eyes and glowing chestnut hair. "Happy housewarming—Ryan style."

He prided himself on surprise attacks. He was inside her kitchen, pulling food out of his basket and uncorking the wine, before she knew what hit her.

"Thought it was high time to properly welcome you to the neighborhood. And what better way than with dinner? On me."

He could tell she wanted to argue. But his offer of dinner was as unthreatening as his carefully schooled manners. He counted on her practical side to see that . . . and to see that not every move he made was fueled by testosterone—which had basically fueled all the moves he'd made to date.

He poured them each some wine and held his glass aloft. She hesitated a moment, then answered his good-natured prompting by doing the same.

"May the hinge of our friendship never grow rusty," he said in his best Irish brogue as they clinked glasses softly.

And may the saints preserve me, Merry prayed silently. What was she letting herself in for? The wildest rogue in all of Ireland, lately of the USA, stood there grinning like the very devil himself. And heaven help her, all she could do was grin back.

"There's a good girl. You're relaxing. See? It's not really so hard to do around me, is it?" he asked, oozing charm and innocence and unassuming sex appeal.

Merry sighed in surrender, leaned a hip against the counter, and took a slow sip of her wine. "You don't quit, do you, Patrick?"

"Oh, the Irish aren't quitters, love. Never have been," he added easily as he rummaged around in her cupboards for a match. Finding one, he lit the broiler. "Hope you like rib-eyes."

"Hmm," she said, not even trying to conjure up a fight.

He flashed her another of those melting grins. "I'll take that as a yes, then."

She quit worrying about the smile she couldn't seem to dampen and watched him go about preparing her dinner.

Merry had a busy week and a long day. She'd barely had time to change from her suit to a soft pink angora sweater and her favorite jeans when she'd heard the knock at her kitchen door.

Her first reaction when she'd seen him standing there had been to send him away. Now she was glad she hadn't. It was nice being catered to. Nice to watch a man who knew his way around a kitchen.

She decided not to think past the moment but to step out on that edge she'd heard so many people talk about. Enjoy it, she told herself, riding on a renegade streak of adventure. It was, after all, only dinner. And the cook had terrific buns.

It turned out to be an enjoyable meal. More so, she thought, because at some point during the day she'd come to terms with what had been happening in her life. Specifically, her life as it related to the dreams. She was tired of being ruled by them.

Admitting that the book was the source of the dreams had been the first step. Confiding in Cory had helped too. Since then Merry had been able to come up with a perfectly acceptable explanation: The romance associated with the book was probably acting as a catalyst for the dreams. Most likely they were triggered by a subconscious attempt of her psyche to complete the portion of her life that lacked a physical as well as an emotional outlet. Simply stated, she was a little lonely. It would pass.

As for the inscription, she admitted it was unusual that it bore her name but persisted in viewing it as a coincidence. Nothing more. As for her impulsive purchase of the house, Cory might find it strange, but Merry didn't.

For thirty-two years she'd been arrow-straight. Hardworking. Focused. She wasn't impulsive. She wasn't reckless. But she had made mistakes. Counting on Gavin had been one of them.

Two years ago, on the heels of their painful divorce, she'd set out to rectify that mistake. She'd reclaimed her maiden name, relocated here in this lovely Eastern Seaboard town, and left behind her unpleasant memories and the insecurities her marriage to Gavin had bred.

It was critical to her that Collectibles be successful, not only for monetary reasons but also because she had something to prove. Not to anyone else, but to herself. She had to prove her own value, to demonstrate that she was strong enough to survive on her own.

The business was off to a good start. But to achieve the financial as well as the personal success she wanted, she had to *work*, to the exclusion of the social side of her life—ergo, romantic dreams and a little restless wanting.

She looked at the man sitting across from her in front of the fire. Patrick posed the final, unanswered question surrounding the book and the dreams. He was a beautiful man. A man any woman would dream about, and in retrospect it was really no big surprise that he just happened to resemble her dream lover.

And tonight didn't have to be such a big deal either, if she'd just relax and bask in the attentions of an attractive, attentive man. He wouldn't become a threat, because she wasn't about to let him. She'd learned her lesson. She'd fallen for a free spirit once— never again.

It was really rather sweet, what he'd done, fixing dinner and all. His insistence that they eat it on the blanket, spread on the floor in front of the fire, had turned it into a playful picnic of sorts.

When he was like this, solicitous, entertaining, and three feet away, he was really very easy to be around. If she discounted the way her heart kicked up when their eyes met, or the way her flesh burned when their fingers accidentally brushed together as they cleared away the dishes.

"That was lovely," she said, leaning back against the settee and establishing that distance again. "Thank you."

He smiled and topped off their wine. "You're very welcome. We'll do it again sometime if you like."

She was afraid that she'd like that very much, she realized, watching the play of muscle beneath his blue-gray sweater as he fed the fire another piece of wood. The man knew how to fill out a sweater. And a pair of jeans, she added silently as he settled in beside her, propping his arm over an upraised knee.

He stared at his wine before meeting her eyes again, his gaze softly questioning.

"It's easier this way, am I right?" he asked.

"Easier?"

While she tried to pretend otherwise, they both knew she understood his question. He was talking about them. About the sexual thunder that had been rumbling around them since they'd first met.

"Easier to put things in the right order," he said softly. "Friends first. Without all the heat. Without all the fire."

But just talking about the fire brought it to flame again. She could feel it sizzling through her veins like a long lit fuse.

"Easier . . ." he repeated in that deep, intoxicating voice. "But not necessarily better."

No, not better, she agreed dismally, and admitted that she'd never experienced anything better than the way she'd felt when he'd held her in his arms the night of the party.

It hit her suddenly that at this very moment she'd like nothing better than to be enfolded in his embrace again. And the notion, instead of startling her, seemed to slip comfortably into place. In fact, it was such a comfortable thought that when he interrupted her musings by tipping her face to his with a gentle pressure of his finger under her chin, she knew she'd been expecting his touch.

"I won't lie to you, Merry. I've known a lot of women."

Glamorous, exotic, worldly women, no doubt, she realized at once. Women who were more than willing to tumble into his arms and into his bed.

"I've always made it clear up front that when it comes to relationships, I don't possess the staying power for anything long-term."

She took a slow sip of wine, knowing he was watching her. Knowing what he was working up to. Wishing that she weren't actually contemplating it herself.

"You've got me rethinking things, love. You intrigue me. Not just physically—though Lord knows the heat generated inside me every time you get within touching distance could fuel a nuclear-power plant."

She couldn't help it. She smiled. Only a fool would deny the chemistry between them, she admitted to herself.

"Besides," he added with a rakish grin, "I found you. In my house, in my bed. That says something, don't you think?"

"Sort of a finders-keepers kind of thing?" she prompted, grinning along with him.

He laughed. A deep, delicious chuckle that warmed her from her head to her toes, including some interesting places in between.

"It's not a question of possession—though any man would fight for the right to possess you. I meant it was like a sign. You were sent to me. All right, so that's stretching it a bit," he conceded, smiling again when he saw the doubtful look in her eyes. "But I do believe in fate. Don't you? Just a little?"

A couple of weeks ago she'd have given him an unqualified no. Considering the events in her life lately, though, she couldn't laugh it off as she'd have liked to. After all, they had been strangers mere days ago; tonight they were sharing something as intimate as fire glow, feelings as rich as chocolate ice cream.

"You feel it, too, don't you?" he asked, reading her thoughts in her eyes. "A connection. A sense that what we could share would be very special."

He touched a hand to her cheek, then, watching her mouth, brushed his thumb gently over her lower lip. The subtly abrasive touch was suggestively intimate and told her what he really wanted to do.

"Since the first time I kissed you, I've spent hours trying to convince myself it wasn't as earth-shattering as I remembered. But it was. Earth-shattering, gut-wrenching, sleep-stealing."

"Yes," she whispered, and heard his sharp intake of breath at her admission that she'd felt it too.

His eyes darkened as he watched her. "So, the question remains, love: What are we going to do about it? I know what I want, but the important thing here, Merry, is what do *you* want?"

Only her dwindling reserves of common sense kept her from throwing herself into his arms and showing him what she wanted. Chemistry, she reminded herself, was not a basis for a relationship, no matter how powerful.

Yet a relationship was the last thing she wanted in her life right now, wasn't it? Relationship implied commitment—and she was wary of making any commitment just now. As she'd too hurtfully learned, commitment could prove to be a one-way street.

But Patrick wasn't talking about a "relationship," was he? He was sugarcoating it a bit, but he was talking about an affair. And affairs didn't require commitment. She rolled the notion around in her head, both thrilled and a bit nettled by his suggestion.

"Forgive me for sounding naive, but no one's ever proposed having an affair to me before. It seems a bit . . . calculated."

"An 'affair'? Your word, Merry, not mine. And put that way, yes, it does sound calculated."

"What else would you call it?"

His gaze dropped again to her mouth. She reacted with an involuntary little shiver.

"I'd call it wanting to get to know you better. I'd call it indulging—and being indulged—in some very basic, very special pleasures. Me pleasing you, you pleasing me. And I find nothing cold or calculating about any of those possibilities."

The fire flickered softly. The faint scent of cedar smoke curled a snug web around them. And the dark eyes probing hers drew on yearnings she'd kept hidden for too long.

She held his gaze for a moment longer than was wise. For in his eyes she saw not only possibilities but a few promises. The combination left her struggling to respond.

She looked toward the fire, knowing she should say anything but what she was about to say. But she was prepared this time, wasn't she? She knew about the flash and the fire. Maybe it was time for her to approach a little slice of her life with the reckless disregard she'd always envied in other people. Besides, this time she knew that neither of them were looking for forever. Just the here and now. The very compelling now.

When she met his eyes again, it was with purpose and poise and a silent plea.

"I want . . ." She hesitated, then, feeling his silent

encouragement, continued, "I want to take this slow."

He watched her carefully before expelling a breath she hadn't been aware he'd been holding.

"Slow," he said at last, repeating the word like an affirmation, recognizing that she was saying yes. Yes to the unknown, and to all the risks that came with it. And she saw in his smile how pleased he was.

"Have you ever heard of an ai?" he asked, taking her hand in his and studying it intently.

"Ai?" She blinked, wondering if she'd missed a part of their conversation.

"An ai is a three-toed sloth," he explained, setting aside his wine, then tucking an errant strand of hair behind her ear in a steady, deliberate motion. "It's the slowest-moving land mammal known to man."

"Ah." She smiled as comprehension dawned, charmed again by the man and by his special way of telling her he'd play by her rules. "You don't say."

"Mm-hmm," he confirmed, his hand lingering to stroke her cheek. "A fast one moves at a ground speed of six to eight feet a minute."

"Ah. Patrick?" she said, tingling with anticipation as she leaned into his caress.

"Hmm?"

"Not that slow."

He smiled, a lazy, slumbrous smile that couldn't quite hide the sensual mischief in his eye. "No?"

"No," she whispered against his lips.

His warm breath feathered across her lips, his rugged, masculine scent set her senses humming. "Then how about I show you how an Irishman sets about handling 'slow'?"

"Yes," she said, as he relieved her of her glass and set it on the floor beside his. "How 'bout you do that."

He showed her then just how slow he could be as he stroked a tantalizing hand over her hair and sent her stomach into a lazy tumble. Showed her how, with a leisurely and luxurious pace, he could draw her deliberately, unerringly, against him. Showed her, when he lowered his head to hers and made lingering, lusty love to her mouth, how to stretch the definition of the word "slow" past all limits, and test her sanity in the process.

He tasted of dark passion and rich red wine as he parted his lips over hers. With delicious languor, he explored her mouth with his tongue. His lips were firm yet incredibly soft, his tongue insistent yet gently probing, as never hurried, never demanding, he romanced her senses with a sizzling combination of nuance and innuendo and desire.

By the time he'd ended the kiss and had drawn her snugly against him, he'd made her a firm believer in the delicacies of languid pleasure. In the aftermath, though, her heart was beating anything but slowly.

She willed her breath to steady as it whispered against his neck in desperate little gasps.

"Lord," Patrick murmured against her hair, struggling to catch his own breath. "This is going to be a challenge."

He'd promised her "slow." She wasn't going to get it at this rate. What she was going to get was more than even he had bargained for. The woman did things to him. Things that fractured his control and begged him to welsh on his promise, honor be damned.

Concentrate, he ordered himself, drawing in deep drafts of head-clearing air. But the air in his immediate vicinity was filled with her . . . with the scent that made her a soft, desirable woman.

He drew her closer. Sobered and shamed by the way she nestled trustingly against him, he stared at the fire and dug deep for something to get him through this without taking her right here on the floor.

Determined, he shifted, ignoring the uncomfortable stirring in his loins. "Speaking of three-toed sloths—"

Her soft laughter cut him off.

"If you think this is easy, love, why don't *you* pick the subject? But pick one quick, or you're going to find out what's really on my mind."

He had no doubt she already knew. Making love. Sweet love. Hot love.

"Maybe we should call it a night," she suggested.

It would have been the smart thing to do, Patrick knew. Where Merry was concerned, however, he was proving to be not very smart at all.

He held her fast. "No. Not yet. I can do this. I promise. Just talk to me. Tell me something. Anything. Tell me about you. What you do. Where you work." *What you're wearing under that soft, crushable sweater*, he added silently, and suppressed a shuddering groan.

He felt her relax as she settled back against him. "There's not much to tell, really. I'm afraid you'd find my life pretty boring compared to yours."

"Merry . . . don't you know by now that everything about you fascinates me? Come on, then. Let's have an earful. Start with your family. Where are they? Are you close?"

"My family is spread all over the country. The folks are still on the farm in Iowa. My brother, Ben, is in L.A. I have a sister, Sarah, in Tennessee."

She tried to conceal it, but he heard her longing for her family. It made her seem more vulnerable, a notion she'd already tried to deny. The fact that she'd deny it again if he suggested it, made him feel protective, which he found both new and oddly pleasant. He stroked a gentle hand up and down the length of her back. "You miss them. I can hear it in your voice."

"Yes. I do miss them. What about you? Do you have family nearby?"

She was purposely redirecting the attention to him. He decided to let her . . . for the moment. "In miles, no, they're not close. But we keep in touch, and I try to squeeze at least one trip home every year."

"And where is home?"

"Sure and begorra, lass," he began, pouring on the brogue as thick as sweet cream, "you must be knowin' that it's Ireland I'm from and Ireland I love."

He felt her smile against his sweater.

"That you're Irish has never been a question. I just

hadn't realized your ties were so close. How did you end up in the States?"

"The truth is, I was born here. My folks have since returned to County Cork, and for several years I lived between there and here. And you, Merry," he asked, suddenly wanting to know everything about her, "how did you end up here?"

She gave a restless shift of her shoulders before answering. "The usual way. After college I got married. His job eventually brought us to Boston. The divorce brought me here."

That didn't sound so usual to him. It sounded painful. For her sake he hesitated, but compelled by a desire to soothe that pain, decided to ask anyway. "Is it something you can talk about?"

She drew in a deep breath, and he sensed that she was considering how much to tell him.

Finally, she answered, "Let's leave it at we both made some mistakes. He wanted different things than I did. When we realized how different, we decided to put the marriage out of its misery."

He'd never felt such a compulsion to console, to shelter, as he ran his hands from her shoulder to her hip, loving the feel of her.

The tension he felt in her body told him the ordeal hurt her more deeply than she'd ever willingly say. And his own tension at the thought of anyone hurting her told him a few things about the depth of his own emotional involvement in her.

She evoked feelings in him he'd never allowed himself to experience before. Had him considering things he'd never thought he could reconcile with the life-style he'd chosen.

And then there was the matter of her divorce. He sensed that commitment was vitally important to her. If she took a vow, she'd fight like the dickens to honor it. Bastards like her ex-husband—bastards like Patrick Ryan who couldn't deal with commitment—were the problem, not her.

Uncomfortable as he was with those conclusions, he still wanted to know more. Yet he acknowledged to himself that he hadn't yet earned the right to know all about her—and, moreover, that he wasn't ready to know some of it. For instance, was the man who had been fool enough to leave her and cruel enough to hurt her still in the picture—his competitor?

"What besides the divorce brought you here?" he asked, steering away from her ex-husband for both of their sakes.

"Economics," she answered easily. "I'd worked for an estate-auction business in Boston, and decided I was ready to start up my own."

"Your own business." He squeezed her lightly, an unauthorized proprietary sense stirring. "I'm impressed. Tell me about it."

She told him eagerly. And judging from the way her eyes lit up, he suspected he'd hit on her one great passion.

"Collectibles deals mostly in antiques. We specialize in handling large estates. Appraisals, auctions, connecting collectors with the right pieces, that sort of thing."

"Hard work?"

"Good work. I enjoy it. Since Cory joined me, it's not as grueling as it was when I first started." She smiled. "For a few months there it looked like I was trying to prove if I actually could meet myself coming and going. Between buying trips, arranging auctions, and book work, I burned a lot of candles. Cory's helped me slow down."

"I think perhaps you still work too hard."

She shrugged off the suggestion. "The hours are sometimes long, that's true. But it's necessary if I want to make it a success. Soon, though, it should get a little better—that is, if I can ever get approval from the zoning commission to base Collectibles in the house. That would save not only on rent, but also on commuting time."

"I hope that means I won't see you burning the midnight oil over here quite as often."

She pulled slowly out of his arms. From under furrowed brows her heather-gray eyes intently met his. "What are you talking about?"

"I'm a restless sleeper, love," he explained, wondering why the rosy glow the fire and the wine had painted on her cheeks had faded to a dusky pink. "I've seen your light on late. In fact, I noticed last night that it was on well past midnight."

Something flashed in her eyes—he'd have sworn he saw desperation, maybe even panic, before they clouded over with what he finally decided was resignation.

As curious as he was disturbed by her reaction, he pushed further before she could recover that poise he found both admirable and infuriating.

"Have you already converted part of the attic into an office then?"

This time there was no mistaking what he saw in her eyes. It was fear. And when she spoke, he heard it in the thready strain of her voice.

"The attic? Why . . . why would you ask that?"

"Because that's where I saw the light, love. In the attic."

Her face went deathly pale.

A chill of unease set all his senses on edge. "Merry?" He framed shoulders that suddenly seemed very fragile beneath his hands. "What is it?"

"I . . ." Her eyes had a wild, trapped look about them as they met his. "I haven't been up in the attic." She looked away, then added in a reedy whisper, "No one's been up there since the electricians replaced some faulty wiring two weeks ago."

SIX

Merry knew she had to get herself under control. And she would—just as soon as she stopped shaking.

Patrick squeezed her shoulders firmly, forcing her to look at him. "Merry, you're as white as a damn sheet. I'm sure there's an explanation for the light. No cause for panic."

He was right. There was a reasonable explanation for the light. She just had to think of one.

But she couldn't think. Not when those dark, probing eyes of his were watching her with such concern. Not when the only explanation within reach went against every logical and rational thought she'd ever had.

She shivered, weakening in her fight to deny that some unexplained phenomenon, some mysterious force that was in some way connected to her dreams, had something to do with what was happening in this house—and in her life.

"Hey now . . . I don't like the looks of this. Is there something going on over here I need to know about?"

Her eyes must have been wild when they met his. He reacted accordingly. "Has someone been bothering you? Have you had a prowler?"

"No, no," she assured him quickly. "I'm sorry. I don't know why I'm acting like this," she lied, aiming for a show of calm. It had been hard enough telling Cory about the dreams. Confiding in Patrick, no matter how compelling the notion seemed at the moment, was something she could not make herself do.

"Look . . . the electricians . . . they must have left the light on," she suggested, forcing a self-censuring smile. Though she was definitely grasping at straws, she warmed to the idea as she developed it. "I . . . I haven't had a chance to go up there since they finished their work. . . . I've been too busy to check things out. That's probably why I haven't noticed it." All of what she said was true, and suddenly a comfort. It was, after all, a viable explanation.

His frown deepened. "All right. That sounds reasonable. But while it might explain the light, it doesn't explain why you were so frightened just now."

"You're right," she agreed, and reached deep to hang on to her smile. "I don't know what came over me. How about we chalk it up to fatigue? It's been a long day."

He seemed to consider that. She could tell he didn't

care much for her explanation, but neither did he want to upset her further.

"Is that your subtle little way of inviting me to leave?" A teasing light had cautiously returned to his eyes.

"Some of us *do* have to work tomorrow," she said, trying for a light, airy tone.

"Uh-oh. It would seem I have a bit of work to do myself."

"Such as?"

"Such as polishing my image as you perceive it." With a resigned sigh he rose to his feet. Backlit by fire glow and shadows, his injured pose was totally staged and utterly disarming.

Grateful that he was letting her steer him away from the subject of the attic, she accepted his proffered hand and let him tug her to her feet.

"Not to worry," she said, smiling. "It's already been polished for you."

He tucked her comfortably under his arm as they walked lazily toward her kitchen. "I don't suppose you'd care to expound on that?"

"It's that free-lance-adventurer image, you know. Shines like gold." She grinned as they bumped hips and squeezed through the kitchen door together.

He groaned and hung his head, managing to nuzzle her neck in the process. "I see Stoner has been vocalizing again. All right, then, I guess there's nothing for it but to hear the tale."

She grinned again at his obvious discomfort. "Max

was much more interested in telling about your exploits than giving me information on the house and bringing the abstract up-to-date. I'm afraid he has a bad case of hero worship."

When Patrick only rolled his eyes, she stopped and looked at him. "He seemed to know an awful lot about you."

"Stoner has been handling this property for the ten years that I've rented the cottage. I guess we've had occasion to talk a few times. He asks a lot of questions. Draws a lot of conclusions."

"I'd guess as much," she said. "My question is, how much of what he told me about you do I believe?"

He looked a bit uncomfortable. "How much do you want to believe?"

Truthfully, she wasn't sure. Max *had* been a talker. Concerned about sealing the deal, she'd only half listened when he'd chattered on about Patrick's globe-trotting adventures and made a sort of veiled insinuation that he was privy to even more information that he couldn't disclose.

"I want to believe what you tell me," she answered finally, and leaned back against the kitchen counter.

He gave a restless shrug before facing her. Draping his wrists with easy familiarity over her shoulders, he cocked his head to one side and looked past her out the window, seemingly considering what he was going to say.

"It's all right," she said, seeing his hesitation. "It's your business, not mine."

"No," he said quickly, shaking his head. "It's not that. It's just that, stated in black and white, it sounds a little juvenile."

"Why don't you try me?"

"Okay," he said after another considering silence. "The essence of it is that I'm a writer. It didn't start out that way, though. After a stint in the Irish equivalent of the army, I went to work for an independent land developer. He needed a troubleshooter to go in to some, shall we say, unexplored political climates and check out potential problems. My experiences working for him whetted my appetite and laid the groundwork for what Stoner likes to refer to as my 'great adventures.' Now I explore on my own, then come back here to set what I've seen and done to paper."

It wasn't as if she hadn't known the truth would be something like that. Hearing about it from him, though, knowing he was living the kind of exciting life Gavin had left her to find brought back the old pain.

She told herself she wasn't disappointed. After all, she couldn't be disappointed, because she wasn't going to let herself become emotionally involved this time. What she and Patrick were cultivating wasn't going to be a lasting relationship. It was going to be . . . something far less.

"So, you write documentaries?" she concluded quietly, working to keep a creeping disappointment out of her voice.

He shook his head and gave her a sheepish look. "Action-adventure novels."

She frowned up at him, puzzled by his look. "Why do I sense you're uncomfortable with that?"

"Oh, Lord, no. I'm not uncomfortable with any of it. I love it. I just didn't want *you* to be uncomfortable with what I do."

She thought about that for a moment. Why did he think it would bother her?

She had a friend in Boston who was a writer. She knew from her struggles that it was the exception, not the norm, to make a living wage in the profession. His rental of the modest cottage also suggested a need to be frugal. Accordingly, she chose her words carefully.

"It's your life, Patrick. Your choice. And the measure here is not how successful you are or how much money you make, but that you're happy doing what you do."

The softest look came over his face. A generous grin followed. "Are you telling me, love, that it doesn't matter to you whether I'm a man of means or just a starving writer who can barely make the rent on a caretaker's cottage?"

Unaccountably warmed by the look in his eyes, she raised her hands to grip the strong forearms propped on her shoulders. "I'm saying money isn't necessarily a yardstick for success."

His smile was soft and intimate. His black eyes glittered invitingly in the dimly lit room. "You've a kind and generous heart, Merry Thomas. Do you suppose there's a wee bit of Irish in you somewhere, lass?"

His words enfolded her in a rosy pocket of pleasure, and she forgot for one moment her resolve not to become emotionally involved with this man. "Sure and you've a block between those devil-black eyes o' yours, Patrick Ryan, if you can't be recognizin' a pure Irish name when yer hearin' one," she replied saucily, surprised at how easily the exaggerated brogue rolled off her tongue.

He threw back his head and laughed, then drew her snugly against him. "Me own ma would be proud, she would, to know that the likes o' me had the good sense to discover a fine Irish lass the likes o' you. Sure an' she would."

Lowering his head, he touched his lips to first one corner of her mouth, then the other. "And she'd never forgive me if I didn't let you know just how lucky I feel. Do you feel it too, Merry?"

"The luck of the Irish?" she asked breathlessly.

"The magic," he whispered, brushing her lips with his own. "Do you feel the magic?"

What she felt was a dizzying rush of sensation as he covered her mouth with his and drew her into a deep, drugging kiss.

And yes, she felt the magic. It had to be magic. What else could explain how he'd taken her from shaking-in-her-shoes scared of an unexplained light to this dazzling sense of aching expectancy? What else could explain why she so readily dropped the guard protecting her heart?

Every time they touched, he lifted her to a new level

of sensual awakening. Every breath they drew in this misty haze of echoing awareness cemented a sense of newness that blended sweetly with familiarity. A sense of fantasy braided with reality and drifted in the background like the ghost of a deep, secret dream.

She clung to him, welcoming the kiss, accepting the power and the pleasure and the need that was mutual and demanding.

On a low, shuddering groan he whispered her name and lifted her onto the counter. His powerful, eager hands skated from shoulder to waist to hip before skimming to her thighs and parting them, claiming the right to move between them.

"Sweet Merry Clare," he whispered hoarsely as she wrapped her legs around his waist and pressed herself against him. His hands tunneled their way under her sweater to stroke her back. "Lord but you're soft . . . and hot. So hot."

She arched into his caress as his mouth tracked greedy, biting kisses from her jaw to her neck before descending to her shoulder.

Need took on an intensity she'd never known when he pulled back and looked into her eyes. His intent was clear. He wasn't asking for permission, he was expecting it. His hands moved to the hem of her sweater.

Trust me, his eyes said. Let me.

Yet despite the searing heat, despite the demand, she knew she could have stopped him with a word. She didn't even try.

Misty-eyed, she lifted her arms in silent admission of the dark, aching need she shared with him.

In a sure, slow motion he tugged the sweater over her head and tossed it aside. Then his hands were in her hair, smoothing it out of her eyes as he dragged her against him for a hard, probing kiss. Those sensual hands then dropped to rest on her shoulders, softly kneading, gently arousing, patiently waiting as he broke the kiss.

The next move, his silence said, was hers. The next move, her heart told her, was irrevocable.

And as she watched the smoky heat in his eyes flare to a crackling blaze, it was her hands, not his, that hesitantly stole to the front clasp of her bra and snapped it open.

Spellbound by the pleasure in his dark gaze as her breasts fell free of satin and lace, she shrugged the straps from her shoulders. Trembling with desire and a newly discovered dimension of her own sexuality, she covered his hands with hers. Slowly, she lowered them to her bared breasts, offering herself with a wantonness she had never shown another man.

His hands were strong yet tender, questing yet rough, as they tested the weight of her breasts, first stroking, then shaping, then cupping as he bent his head and drew a distended nipple into his mouth.

She shivered and leaned into the sweet tugging sensation as he suckled one breast while reverently kneading the other.

"You taste like heaven itself," he murmured, extending her pleasure with teasing nips, scraping nuzzles, and long, lazy suckling.

"My God, Patrick," she gasped, burying her hands in his hair as he moved from one exquisitely sensitized breast to the other.

"Heaven," he repeated. Then, tearing himself away, he drew her hard and fast against him.

She sucked in a harsh breath at the fierceness of his embrace, at the delicious scrape of his wool sweater against the sensitive tips of her swollen nipples.

"Lord, girl." He drew in a deep draft of air. "This is a far, far cry from slow."

Pacing, however, was no longer her priority. Need had replaced it. Joy in her rediscovered awareness of herself as a woman had outdistanced caution.

She'd been lonely long before the divorce. Self-preservation had forced her to pack her sexuality at the bottom of her emotional trunk. It had taken the dreams of Jamie to make her aware that it still existed. It had taken the reality of Patrick to make her want to unpack it, air it out, and try it on again to see if it still fit.

But a long, hard look at where this was leading made her realize that too much too soon could be more damaging than waiting until the time was right.

She sighed in frustration. Regret and need grappled with control for the upper hand.

"Not to worry, love," he whispered. "It's okay. And this will go no farther. Not tonight."

She turned her face against his chest. "It seems I'm always underestimating you."

"Underestimating me?" His breath feathered across the top of her head.

"Who would have thought it would be you who would step back and recognize this is going too fast for me? I'm sorry," she whispered in apology and thanks, brushing her mouth against his neck.

He rocked his gently. "Nothing to be sorry for."

She realized then just how special this man could be. "Most men wouldn't see it that way. Most men would be damn mad that I started something I'm not quite ready to finish."

"Make no mistake, Merry: I'm the one who started it. And I knew when I did there would be a limit."

He tried to pull away to look at her. She held him fast, painfully aware that the only thing covering her naked breasts was his chest. Achingly aware that she was vulnerable to this man as she'd never been to another.

Sensing her sudden shyness, he twisted, reached around her, and found her sweater. Never letting her go, he managed to settle it over her head.

"You . . . you continue to amaze me," she said when she'd squirmed into the garment.

She felt his smile form against the top of her head. "I sincerely hope so." He set her gently away. "Now, if I don't take my Irish self out of here this very minute, I'm going to get lost again in those soft, yearning eyes of yours and forget everything I ever knew about three-toed sloths. G'night, love," he whispered after a lingering, lengthy kiss. "Sweet dreams." Then he slipped quickly out her kitchen door.

As it turned out, Merry hardly slept, let alone dreamed. The old house seemed less settled than usual, full of distant little creaks in the night that added to her own restless yearning for Patrick . . . and her gnawing unease about the light in the attic. Patrick had offered to go upstairs and check it out for her, but she'd begged off, telling him she'd take care of it in the morning. The truth was, she didn't want to deal with it tonight . . . didn't want to face another unknown.

It had to be the electricians, she repeated like a mantra as she wrestled a pillow over her ears to shut out the sounds of the house's subtle shiftings. Or the moon. Yes, that was probably it—just a case of the full moon reflecting through the windows. And maybe it was the moon making her lose sight of her resolve to avoid anything but a physical involvement with Patrick.

Whatever the reasons, they were further complicated the next morning. After two cups of coffee and several deep, bracing breaths, she worked up the nerve to confront the attic light.

The only problem was, she couldn't get into the attic because the door was locked. And the key to the door—which she could have sworn was on the master ring with all the other keys—had mysteriously vanished. When a thorough search of both upstairs and down didn't produce the key, she gave up the search in puzzled frustration and headed for the office.

She was still struggling with the key's perplexing disappearance when she decided to call work quits at noon. It was Saturday, after all. She needed a break. It was a beautiful day, and she wanted to be a part of it. Besides, guilt got the best of her. Cory had shown up at the office and insisted on working right alongside her. Merry knew from experience that if she didn't pack it in, neither would Cory.

By one o'clock Merry was sweeping leaves from the wraparound front porch, enjoying the autumn sunshine and the crisp nip in the air, when she spotted Cory's red compact tooling up the street.

"I thought I sent you home to wax your legs . . . or was it your floors?"

"Neither. I had more important things to do." Cory slanted her a secretive smile as she slammed out of the driver's side of her car, wrestling with an armload of books. "So . . . how's it going?"

Thinking about her quick and futile hunt for the missing attic key before she'd given up in favor of some fresh air, Merry shrugged. "I guess that's open for debate." Walking down the steps to meet Cory, she relieved her of some of the books. "What's all this?"

"Research. Now don't get mad," Cory added hurriedly when Merry scowled over one title, then another. "These just might lend a little insight to your situation."

"*The Theory of Paranormal Phenomena . . . Back*

From Beyond . . . Channeling in the Nineties." Merry groaned. "Come on, Cory. I told you I don't buy this stuff."

"Whether you buy it or not isn't going to make it go away. I figure you might find some answers in these."

"I need answers, but I'm not going to find them in these books," Merry insisted.

Looking up, she saw Cory was staring past her, a puzzled smile on her face.

Merry followed Cory's gaze and smiled, too, when she spotted the little girl standing at the end of the sidewalk leading to the porch steps. The child stared alternately at Merry and then at the house in utter silence, looking ready to bolt at the least provocation.

She couldn't have been more than six or seven, Merry decided. Big brown eyes, a waist-long honey-gold ponytail, and scuffed sneakers made a charming contrast to the lavender T-shirt and jeans and the rag doll tucked protectively under her arm.

"Hi," Merry said, waving.

The brown eyes grew bigger. The sneakers shuffled a little but stayed put.

"My name is Merry. This is my friend Cory. What's your name?"

"Do you really live in there?" came an awed response.

"Well, yes, I just moved in," Merry said with a friendly smile. "Does that make us neighbors?"

The child cast a nervous glance down the street. Merry could only guess that she was looking toward home, since her own property was at the end of a dead-end street and so overgrown with shrubs and trees that she might as well be in the middle of a forest.

"Have . . . have you seen the ghost yet?" the child asked, her eyes as wide and round as twin moons.

"Ghost?" Cory echoed, her ears perking up. "There's a ghost? I *knew* there had to be a ghost."

"Cory, for heaven's sake," Merry sputtered when she saw the fear in the little girl's eyes. "Of course there's no ghost."

"My sister says there is. She says your house is *haunted*," the child blurted out. And then quite obviously scaring herself by the declaration, she ran down the street and out of sight.

Before Merry could fully absorb the little girl's blunt statement, she caught Cory's dark expression. She was gearing up to say "I told you so."

"I don't want to hear it," Merry warned her, then glanced uneasily down the street in the direction the child had run. "She's an impressionable little girl, and this is a big old house. Old house, haunted house. They equate to one and the same where children's imaginations are concerned."

"If you say so," Cory agreed in an irritatingly condescending tone.

Despite the unexplained lights in the attic, Merry was ready to defend her position. Then she noticed Cory's gaze drifting past her head again. Interest and an unmistakable spark of excitement colored Cory's cheeks and widened her expressive eyes.

"This seems to be your day for company," Cory said, smiling brightly. "Don't look now," she continued in a low voice, the episode concerning the ghost clearly forgotten, "but your tenant seems to have decided to pay you a visit. And isn't he sweet—he's brought along a little playmate for me."

Merry whipped her head around. Sure enough, Patrick was working his way around the side of the house. The "little playmate" had long blond hair and appeared to be about six and a half feet of herculean muscle draped in snug painter pants and a T-shirt that might have hung loosely on Don Knotts. On this man, however, brawn was busting out all over.

"If he can spell his name," Cory whispered, fanning herself as though she were about to faint, "I think I'm in love."

Merry wrestled the rest of the books from Cory and shoved them discreetly behind a porch railing. "Patrick, hello."

He smiled—a lazy, intimate smile that started a blush in her cheeks before spreading down her neck to her breasts, which tingled and tightened beneath her red sweater.

"I'm glad to see you knocked off work early today," he said. *And I haven't stopped thinking about the way you tasted last night,* his eyes added silently.

"Well, you know what they say," she said huskily. "All work and no play . . ."

Sunlight glinted off jet-black hair that a gentle breeze had ruffled like a careless lover. And despite the emotional risk that went with it, she wanted to be that lover, Merry admitted without shame and with a streak of recklessness that made her feel both alive and new.

He was a beautiful man. If he'd been decked out in a tailored tux right now instead of faded jeans and a slate-gray sweatshirt, he couldn't have looked more gorgeous.

Cory cleared her throat. Loudly.

"Oh, I'm sorry." Snap out of it, Merry, she ordered herself, dragging her gaze away from Patrick and her thoughts away from last night and what had happened between them. "Patrick, you remember Cory from the party?"

He grinned at her, then at Cory. "Right. How's it going?"

"Well. It's going very well." Cory smiled for Patrick, but her eyes were only for the Viking warlord. "I don't think we've met."

Patrick made the introductions.

"What an unusual name," Cory purred, floating down the steps to bask in a pair of blue Scandinavian eyes. "Can you spell that for me?"

Merry rolled her eyes as the new kid on the block grinned and politely spelled out *J-E-R-R-Y*.

Unapologetic, Cory flashed him a winning smile. Jerry, unaware that he'd passed a test that had elevated him to marriage material, smiled back as Cory launched into a conversation that was tailor-made for two.

Merry was so in awe of how fast Cory had staked a claim that Patrick's hand on her arm startled her.

"I think I just lost my racquet ball partner."

"I think I don't believe what I just saw."

He laughed. "Seems to be a lot of heavy-duty chemistry hovering around this place. Speaking of chemistry," he added, cupping her elbow and propelling her up the steps and into the privacy of the foyer, "I'd like to put a little equation to the test right now." He closed the door behind them and effectively shut out the rest of the world.

"Equation?" She smiled up into eyes so full of mischief and mirth that she found it impossible to feel self-conscious about what was happening between them.

"Mmm-hmmm. The goal," he began, "is combustion. In theory, I think I know how to make it happen. In practice, however, it needs a little more testing."

"Well . . ." She grinned coyly as she leaned back against the door and played along. "Are you going to theorize all day, or are you planning on putting it to the test?"

Moving unerringly toward her, he braced his forearms on either side of her head and pressed her against the door with his body. She closed her eyes, relishing the heat and the weight and the pressure he stirred low in her belly as he whispered soft, silken kisses over her face, starting with her eyelids working slowly toward her mouth.

"Hello," he said softly when he'd sipped and savored his fill. "How are we doing?"

She sighed deeply. "I think we're close to flash point."

He chuckled, a low, sexy rumble that added to the warmth in her belly and the weakness in her knees. She clutched the doorknob with one hand and a handful of his sweatshirt with the other to keep from slithering to the floor.

"Let's see what we can do about igniting that spark."

It was a slow, searing ignition as he slanted his mouth over hers, infusing the kiss with a lethal combination of lips and teeth and tongue.

They were both breathing hard when he ended the kiss. Any thought of proceeding with caution had long since been factored out of the equation.

"Had I known chemistry could be this, ah, stimulating," she managed between breaths, "I'd have signed up for the course back in high school. Do I smell smoke?" she added, feeling weightless and aching and burning up with desire.

A corner of his mouth tipped up. "Yes, and if we don't curtail this little chemistry lesson, you're also going to see some fire." He dropped a cool-down kiss on her forehead. "And on that note, we'd better go see what Jerry and Cory are up to. We came over with the intent of helping with a little yard work. He may, at this moment, be knee deep in oak leaves."

"Or running scared. I've never seen Cory like this."

"Jerry can handle himself, believe me. But just for fun, let's go see how they're doing."

She'd have liked nothing better than to leave the leaves to Jerry and Cory and to get on with the chemistry class. But with her hand in his, she followed him out the door, praying the effect of their kiss didn't show.

The amused look on Cory's face squashed that hope in a heartbeat. Ignoring her smirk, Merry grabbed a rake and joined in on the work in progress.

The four of them spent the rest of the afternoon working and playing in the brisk autumn sunshine and falling leaves. Once she got past thinking of Jerry in terms of greasing his body and posing him under a strobe light, Merry found a lot to like about him.

Contrary to the physical image he presented, he was charmingly shy and unassuming, surprising her regularly with a dry wit and boyish smile. As the day unfolded, she was firmly parked in Cory's corner, rooting the budding relationship on.

They ended the day as naturally as it had evolved, by grilling burgers, then sipping wine and roasting marshmallows over a blaze in the fireplace.

Cory and Jerry had taken to each other the way mallards take to water. Neither of them were of a mind to deny the attraction. Nestled together on the sofa, they alternately watched the fire and whispered like teenagers at a movie.

As for herself, Merry had long since given up the

pretense that there was nothing going on between herself and Patrick. They had settled on the floor, Patrick leaning comfortably against the settee with her wedged between his legs, her back against his chest. For the moment she chose to enjoy rather than question how fast things were happening.

The mood was mellow, the fire crackling and warm. So when the few lights that were on suddenly went out, it took a moment before any of them mustered the energy to react.

Cory was the first to speak. "Is this the part where bells, books, and candles start flying across the room?"

"Cory . . ." Merry warned.

"Well . . . you heard what that little girl said."

"Cory . . ." Merry repeated, with more feeling this time.

"What's she talking about, love?" asked Patrick, shifting positions as he set her away from him so he could see her face.

"She's talking gibberish . . . and doing it quite well, I might add."

"I'm talking," Cory state deliberately, "about a little girl who came calling just before you two showed up this afternoon. She told us that this house is haunted."

Merry clamped her mouth shut and started a slow burn.

She felt Patrick's gaze on her face and stared stubbornly at the fire.

"And you believed her?" he asked quietly.

"Of course I didn't believe her. And Cory didn't believe her either, did you, Cory?" Merry said, the message clear that if Cory wanted to keep her job, she'd let the subject die a quick, painless death.

"Guess not," Cory grumbled, then screamed as a sharp rap cracked into the silence like a great rattling chain. Eyes wide, she clambered onto Jerry's lap.

"I think I'd like to take you to see a Stephen King movie," said Jerry, chuckling as Cory squirmed as close as she could get without actually crawling inside his sweater.

"What was that?" Cory cried.

"It could have been one of a hundred things," Merry insisted. "A branch brushing a window, a bird flying against the house . . ."

"The shutter on the window above the kitchen sink," Patrick added with a calming voice. "I noticed it today when we were raking. It's loose. Just the right little skiff of wind could set it shaking."

"That doesn't explain the lights," Cory insisted again, wrapping herself around a perpetually grinning Jerry.

"Come on, Jer," Patrick said, rising. "Pry yourself loose, and let's go find the breaker box."

"You're not actually going to leave us here alone," Cory wailed as the men headed toward the basement.

"Cory, will you just stop?" Merry sputtered. "We

blew a fuse. That's all. They'll replace it, and that will be the end of it."

Cory wasn't buying it. "Have you told him about the dre—"

Merry clamped a hand over Cory's mouth, cutting her off.

Patrick paused at the door. "Told me about what?"

"About the flashlight," Merry said quickly, slicing Cory a warning glare. "It's in the kitchen, under the sink. You'll need it if you're going down to the basement."

He looked at her strangely for a moment, then, placated by her smile, headed for the kitchen, with Jerry right behind him.

Several minutes later, when the men returned to the living room, the house was still dark. Merry was scowling at the fire. Cory was perched tensely on the edge of the settee, alternately clicking the heels of her red sneakers together and chanting, "There's no place like home, there's no place like home. . . ."

"I don't understand it," Patrick said, flashing the beam from the flashlight into the room. "Everything's in order down there. Maybe we should check out the attic."

He'd barely gotten the words out of his mouth when the lights flickered, then came to life just as mysteriously as they'd died.

Merry met his puzzled scowl across the room, unable to quell a growing sense of unease. The instant he'd mentioned going up to the attic, the lights had come on.

"Loose wires?" she suggested feebly.

He shrugged. "Beats the hell out of me. First thing Monday morning, though, I want you to call an electrician . . . and not the one who did the original work for you. Right now I'm not feeling too confident about what's been done to date. First they leave lights on where you don't want them, and then you have no lights at all."

"What lights? What lights did they leave on?" asked Cory, her gaze skating from Merry to Patrick.

"Cory, it's no big thing. They left a light on in the attic. It's taken care of. I shut it off this morning."

The moment she'd said it, Merry knew she'd made a mistake.

Cory's gaze snapped to Merry, ready to dispute her statement. She clamped her mouth shut and grudgingly kept her silence, though, when she read Merry's pleading look.

Merry let out a pent-up breath, grateful that Cory, for once, had shown some tact. Merry couldn't have shut off the light and Cory knew it, because she'd overheard Merry call the electrician from the office that morning. She'd heard every detail as Merry had explained that she couldn't find the key to her attic before asking him if there was a chance he had taken it with him when he'd finished the work two weeks ago.

Cory also knew the electrician's answer had been no, he didn't have the key.

Merry cast a worried look toward the attic, praying Patrick didn't catch her in her little white lie. Praying that the light stayed off—or that she could figure out what to tell Patrick if it mysteriously came on again.

Tomorrow, she'd look for the key. Again.

SEVEN

While they couldn't agree on the cause of the power outage, they all agreed it was getting late.

Standing on the front porch, Merry and Patrick watched Jerry's taillights disappear down the street, followed by Cory's.

Patrick folded her in his arms from behind. She leaned back against him, fending off the chill of the crisp autumn night and the niggling unease that a growing list of unexplained occurrences had bred. It no longer surprised her that seeking the shelter of his arms seemed as natural as breathing.

"I thought they'd never leave," he said into her hair.

She smiled. "You don't mean that."

"I do."

Chuckling at his bluntness, she snuggled deeper into his warmth. "Well, I must admit that as much as I enjoyed their company, it has been a long day."

They watched the stars for a moment, sharing a comfortable silence before she spoke again. "I don't think they quite know what to do about each other."

"Those two? Ha. They know exactly what to do. And on that note . . ." He turned her in his arms to face him. "There's something I've been wanting to do all night."

"All night?"

Leaning back against the porch railing, he tugged her with him, linking his arms around her waist. "All night."

For a long, searching moment he looked into her eyes. "I think I've got it bad, love," he confessed on a gruff whisper. "I have to kiss you, you know. There's just no stopping the notion."

He lowered his head slowly, his mouth covering hers with incredible tenderness. Made sweeter by his care, made poignant by his control, his kiss combined devastating measures of desire and restraint, enticement and withdrawal. Merry's response was total submission. She opened her mouth eagerly to his irresistible invasion, falling deeper and deeper under the spell he was spinning.

When she was with him, when she was touching him, when he was touching her, the thought that enveloped her was not that she should send him away, but how right he made her feel. How right it was to be with him. How right the world seemed when she was in his arms.

Secret dreams, mysterious inscriptions, unexplained lights, and disappearing keys all ceased to matter.

When she was with him.

She was with him now. And God help her, with the moonlight as her witness and the falling leaves to whisper encouragement, she knew that tonight she wanted him to stay.

That admission should have shocked her. It didn't. The notion had been there, prowling the edge of her consciousness like a silent, diligent guard, since the morning she'd awakened to find him watching her. While she'd been busy denying it and trying to protect her heart, he'd been stealthily crawling inside it. Storming her with sensory pleasures, warming her with clever words, he'd shown her what it could be like if she'd only take the chance.

Life was a risk. And Patrick Ryan was a risk worth taking.

"Regarding the matter of pace," she began, when their mouths parted.

Burying his face against her throat, he nuzzled her sweetly. "Not to worry, love. I made a promise. I'm thinking sloth."

She smiled and touched a hand to his jaw, bringing his head up. The bold lines of his face were enticingly shadowed by darkness, beautifully haloed by moonglow. "I was thinking . . . maybe it would be a good idea to *pick up* the pace a bit."

His eyes softened, then darkened as if he were afraid to believe he'd understood her meaning. He

smoothed the hair back from her brow with an unsteady hand. "A bit?"

His characteristic show of uncertainty was the gentle nudge she needed. She raised on her tiptoes and
kissed him—not the restrained, tentative kiss of a fragile, timid lover, but a passionate kiss, telling in its
urgency. A kiss a woman gives a man. A kiss a man
recognizes as an invitation.

The sudden hammering of his heart against her
breast told her he'd gotten the message.

Reluctant to end the contact, she sucked gently on
his lower lip, then scraped it between her teeth with a
provocative tug before slowly pulling away.

Anticipation threaded a husky, seductive promise
through her whisper. "What's the fastest land mammal
known to man?"

He swallowed hard as she nipped his chin, scattering lazy, lingering kisses along the shadowed length of
his jaw. "The cheetah."

"Think cheetah," she whispered, and felt a shudder
ripple through his body.

He gripped her hard by the shoulders and set her
away so he could see her face. The look that stormed
his eyes was primal and possessive, and as predatory as
the sleek, fast cat in question. "You're sure?" His voice
had grown gruff with need.

In that moment she was sure of only one thing: She
wanted to make love with him. She suspected, too, that
if she let herself, she could even fall a little in love with
him. She didn't like the idea, didn't intend to let it take

root. But as he stood there, his body poised and straining, yet determined to back away if she said the word, she really didn't have a choice as to how this night would end.

He talked a good game, Patrick Ryan did. He played the flirt, he played the predator. But in matters of the heart, in matters of *her* heart, he put his own needs on hold to offer her every chance to protect it.

"Stay with me, Patrick. I want you to stay with me tonight."

With a sound that coupled a victorious growl with joyous laughter, he scooped her into his arms. "Try to make me leave now, love. Just try it and see what it gets you."

He kissed her again, soundly. "Where to?"

She wound her arms around his neck as an electric excitement arrowed through her body. "First room, top of the stairs."

They didn't quite make it to the room. They barely made it into the foyer. Kicking the door closed behind them, he set her down, letting her slide, inch by treasured inch, down the length of his body. It was a slow glide, a shared seduction designed to create and nurture a building conflagration of straining flesh and merging heat.

With his hands at the hem of her sweater, tugging it up and over her head, he backed her toward the wall. Flattening her against it with his hips, he pressed his arousal in a blatantly erotic message against the cradle of her thighs. When she found his hips with her hands and pulled him closer, his hand went unerringly to the front clasp of her bra.

"I haven't been able to get you out of my mind," he whispered, peeling the brassiere aside and stripping it down her arms. "Seeing you in my bed that first morning and knowing I couldn't touch you was torture."

As if he couldn't wait a moment longer, he bent his dark head to her breasts, drawing her deeply into his mouth.

She gasped, tangling her hands in his hair and holding him against her. His hunger fostered a gnawing ache deep in the essence of everything that made her a woman.

"Last night," he murmured, pressing wet, devouring kisses to her breasts. "The hardest thing I've ever done was leaving you last night."

She cried out when he bit her lightly, then soothed the exquisite hurt with the lavish caress of his hands and tongue.

"Patrick . . . please . . ." A restless urgency stole her breath and her patience. "Hurry."

He pulled her away from the wall and lifted her against him again. She wrapped her legs around his waist, tugging on his sweatshirt, managing, finally, to strip it over his head and fling it aside as he walked them toward the stairs. With a feline sigh, she pressed her breasts against his bare chest, loving the contact of heated skin on heated skin.

Snagging her hands in his hair, she yanked his mouth down to hers with a groan of victory.

"Sweet Lord," Patrick growled, and giving in halfway up the stairs, laid her down, covering her body with his. "At this rate we'll never make it to the bed, love," he whispered with a laugh that was loving and lusty and gravelly with need.

"At this rate I'll die of frustration." She reached for him when he rolled to his hip and away from her. "Come back."

"Shhh." He touched her cheek to settle her, then watched his hand descend to stroke her throat before lowering it to seduce a breast. "You are so beautiful, Merry. Like ivory and lace and rose petals. The only thing I love more than looking at you is touching you."

Watching her eyes, he unfastened the snap of her jeans, then eased them down her hips. She toed off her shoes as he peeled the soft denim down her legs.

Totally vulnerable to him now, her senses came alive with stunning awareness. Cold, hard oak, unyielding beneath hot, bare skin. Cool midnight air whispering across her pebbled nipples. A callused, possessive hand skillfully caressing her belly.

And then his hand was there, where she needed him most, cupping her through a thin layer of satin and lace, making her writhe, making her moan.

"Patrick, please," she begged, stilling his hand. "I want to be with you. I want to touch you. . . ."

With her last shred of self control, she rose to her feet. She took his hands and urged him to get up too.

When he was standing tall and dangerously aroused beside her, she descended a step. Locking eyes with his, she faced him at chest level and unfastened his fly with trembling hands. Thrilled anew by the brush of her fingers against the dark, curling hair on his lean belly, she explored him with lingering pleasure.

He groaned and loosely knotted his hands in her hair. When she pressed her mouth to his chest, tasting him for the first time, he shuddered and fought for control. But when she knelt to slip his jeans down his hips and strip them from his thighs, he lost his tenuous hold. Swearing under his breath, he dragged her to her feet. Kicking free of his jeans and shoes, he scooped her into his arms again.

She was floating, free-falling, weightless in his arms as he ate up the remaining stairs two at a time. He reached the hall, picked a door, and stopped in front of it. At her dazed nod of confirmation, he shouldered it open.

In that room, in her bed, the sensations began again.

So many . . . so fast . . . so exquisite. She wanted to savor each one, yet recklessly release it and go on to the next delicious assault on her senses.

Eyelet lace and goose-down softness rustled against her back.

Masculine weight and the impossibility of heated steel sheathed in sleek satin pressed her into the mattress.

A musky male scent and midnight desire drifted in the air like the mist of a recurrent dream.

His mouth moved over hers in a blatant claim, a

defiant possession. *You're mine*, he said without words. *Trust me . . . trust yourself to me. To feel. To experience. To love.*

And she did trust. And she did love. She relished the brush of his lips on her breast. The caress of his mouth on her belly. The gentle probing of his tongue at the sensitive flesh defining her as a woman who was liquid with desire for this man.

She whispered his name. He took her deeper. She chanted a plea. He showed no mercy. And when she breathlessly cried out in surrender . . . he selflessly set her free.

Devastating, thought-stealing pleasure sluiced through her body in slow, sultry waves. Silken pleasure engulfed her. Patrick's essence surrounded her. And when his satin-black eyes impaled her, she opened herself completely, beckoning him, please, to come home.

Patrick hovered above her, peripherally aware that his arms were trembling with his need for her. She was incredible. So pure in her self-expression. So open to her own desires. And so ready to give back full measure.

She reached for him, caressing him boldly with her small hands. Her touch pushed him close to the edge. Inside his body a fire raged. Inside his head desire fueled obsession. Desperately fighting both, he made himself face his responsibility.

He murmured his concerns for her protection. She whispered husky assurances . . . then begged him to become one with her, her trust in him implicit in her lack of hesitation.

Filled with awe and humility and a promise to himself not to hurt her, he gathered her in his arms.

"Please," she whispered, demonstrating her urgency by the sharp thrust of her nails into his back.

Covering her with his body, he took what she so generously offered with one deep, explosive thrust. She cried out and clung to him. He captured her mouth with his, muffling her exultant cry with a claim as physical as it was sensual as her slim body clenched around him in the sweetest kind of agony.

Nothing had ever felt this good. Nothing had ever seemed so right. He filled her again and again, the reality of being inside her better than any fantasy he could possibly have imagined.

She was heat. She was heaven. She was shivery sighs and sultry moans, wild with desire, wanton with discovery.

She was a dream he hadn't known he harbored, a haven that told him he was home.

And as his body convulsed to the ultimate mind-stealing end, he knew also that she was his. That she was meant to be his. Always. Forever. She was the part of him he had never known he'd been missing . . . because until Merry, he hadn't known what he had lost.

Early-morning sunshine filtered through Merry's bedroom window, kissing the dark lashes that shielded the eyes of the man who watched her with flashes of gold.

She closed her eyes and drifted. "There's something the Irish are noted for besides luck, I see."

"And what might that be, love?" His voice was sleep-rough and husky, as seductive as a sea breeze on a hot summer day.

"Stamina."

He chuckled and pulled her snugly against him. "You're complaining, then?"

She sighed. "I'm complaining now. I don't think I can walk."

He came up on an elbow, searching her face with concern.

She touched a hand to his cheek and smiled a lazy assurance that said, *Yes, I'm teasing . . . yes, I'm okay . . . and yes, last night was incredible. . . .*

"Incredible," however, didn't begin to cover it. She'd thought nothing could compare to the first time they'd come together. She'd been wrong. He'd loved her again and again during the night. Each time, like the time before it, was beyond compare. Alternately tender, alternately fierce, he'd taken her to the fringe of sensation, then tumbled her over the edge.

Basking in his lazy lover's gaze and the haze of latent passion, Merry stretched her arms above her head and squirmed deeper into the mattress. She couldn't remember ever feeling this totally and thoroughly exhausted. This completely and irreverently sated.

The man responsible for the languor and the laziness grinned. "You look like the cat that lapped all the sweet cream, love."

She stretched again, arching against the sheets, clasping her hands higher above her head, and rewarded him with a feline purr. "I suppose you'd like to take credit?"

His chuckle was wicked and smug as he peeled back the sheet and looked at her. "I'd rather take you," he whispered.

His eyes glittered with arousal as they leisurely explored the arch of her breasts with their shell-pink nipples, the concave hollow of rib to belly, the flare of her woman's hips, the soft nest of curls that sheltered her femininity.

Despite the exertions of that night, despite the improbability, she gripped the spindles of the headboard as a subtle stirring, a sleepy reawakening, eddied through her.

His eyes met hers in silent communication while his hand tracked the same path as his visual journey.

"How do you do this to me?" she whispered, awed by the depth of her reactions.

Rising above her, he knelt between her thighs, running his hands in a satin caress from her ankles to her upraised knees. Watching her face, he dropped a kiss on one knee, then the other, as his nimble, magical fingers touched and stroked and adored.

"Do you want me to stop?" he murmured when her heartbeat quickened.

She opened her mouth but managed only a groan as a dark hand swallowed a breast and kneaded gently.

How did she ever get so lost in him? she asked herself, then ceased to wonder, ceased to care, as he lifted her hips to his and drew her under again.

The wreckage was as total as she'd suspected. Wrapped in a red satin robe, Merry tiptoed from the bedroom and beheld the scene of the crime.

She couldn't help but chuckle, then checked herself so as not to awaken the perpetrator, who was snoring quite wonderfully in her bed.

His jeans, shoes, and socks lay tumbled and tossed in scattered disarray down the length of the stairs. His sweatshirt hung drunkenly on the newel post, while pieces of her clothing lay haphazardly across the landing and trailed a path to the door.

She gathered items as she went, blushing though she hadn't thought she had a blush left in her as she spotted her bra hanging brazenly from the doorknob.

"Kids," she muttered with a self-chiding grin.

And that's exactly how she felt, she realized, hugging his sweatshirt to her face. Like a kid. Happy and innocent and new.

Innocent. As out of context as that word seemed in conjunction with what had transpired in her bed last night, she clung to it just the same.

There had been an innocence in the way she'd given

herself to him. In the trust and openness with which she'd expressed her need.

The blush returned. While she had considered herself a sensual person, she'd expanded the concept of sensuality by light-years last night.

Patrick . . . Patrick had made her so aware of herself as a woman. And so aware of him as a man. Awareness had added power to her perceptions and strength to her growth. And a boldness she hadn't known she possessed.

But in spite of it all, yes, she still felt like an innocent. Innocent in the knowledge that she had never felt this way before.

Innocent, or naive? she asked herself as reality nullified some of her pleasure. Remember who he is, she told herself sternly. Remember what he is.

Remember this isn't forever.

Sobered by those warnings, she walked to the kitchen, automatically going through the motions of brewing coffee and starting breakfast.

The bacon was just beginning to curl when she sensed his presence in the room.

She steeled herself for a clumsy morning-after hello.

"Good"—her breath caught, then flooded slowly from her lungs as she turned to fully face him— "morning," she finished, unable to dampen an incredulous smile as he joined her gloriously naked and fully aroused.

"Not good. The best," he insisted, expanding on

her sentiment as he closed the distance between them and took her in his arms.

It was hard for a woman to nurture depression when a man looked at her the way this man was looking at Merry now.

"Did you know," she murmured as he backed her up against the refrigerator and tugged on the belt of her robe, "that you have a decidedly repetitive penchant for pinning me against doors and walls and . . ." She caught her breath as he bent to nuzzle her jaw and peel the robe from her shoulders.

"Other hard things?" he finished for her, sipping his way back to her mouth.

Behind her back, the cold metal of the refrigerator door penetrated the thin satin of her robe. Against her stomach, the searing heat of his arousal diffused the chill.

"The bacon," she whispered as he lifted her, wrapped her legs around his waist, and settled her onto his heat.

"I like it burned," he growled, and gripping the counter on either side of the refrigerator for leverage, he ground himself deep inside her.

He groaned. She gasped. The motor hummed. The bacon burned. And during it all the refrigerator vibrated through their senses complementing the rhythm of their lovemaking.

"Lord," he murmured when he could form a word.

Breathing hard, sanity slowly returning, she managed a distant "Amen."

"Merry?"

"Hmmm?"

He pressed an exhausted kiss to her forehead. "Don't ever sell this refrigerator."

She collapsed against him, her sated chuckle muffled against his chest as she unwrapped her legs and slipped bonelessly to the floor.

Patrick wasn't sure he would ever get used to looking at her. It had been one thing to imagine the texture of the skin beneath her clothes. It was another to know its silken substance. To know what it felt like to caress her with his mouth, to have her take him deep inside her.

But there were limits. Even for a smitten Irishman.

After a leisurely breakfast—she'd made him cook fresh bacon—they'd shared a nap in the huge claw-foot bathtub adjacent to her bedroom. Neither had been capable of anything else. But he was holding the thought and had some specific ideas that he was sure she would improve upon the next time they had an itch to get squeaky-clean together.

Not stopping to question why he felt this sense of urgency, he left her only long enough to sprint home to change into clean jeans and sweater and snag her Sunday paper from the front porch.

That's when he spotted the books, tucked secretively behind a column on the porch floor.

He scooped them up, rifling through the titles as he let himself in the front door.

"What's all this, love?" he asked, settling onto the sofa beside her.

She glanced up from the work she'd brought home and had insisted she had to go over before the day was through. When she saw the books in his arms, her eyes hardened. Just as quickly, though, she smiled, and he wondered if he'd imagined the momentary unease he'd sensed.

"Cory must have forgotten to take them with her," she said casually—too casually, he thought—and went back to reviewing her work.

Scowling, he thumbed through *Back From Beyond* while she, in his estimation, worked overhard at ignoring the book in his hand.

He traded that book for another. "Cory's into this kind of stuff, then?"

She shrugged. "If it slips over the edge, it'll spark Cory's interest—at least for a little while. This week it's the paranormal. Next week it could be sumo wrestling."

"Interesting," he mused aloud, "that she brought them to you."

She glanced up at him. With a nervous little twitch of her lips, she returned her attention to the account books in her lap, choosing to ignore the implication that Cory had brought the books for Merry's benefit.

He frowned as he perused the next book, trying to

key in to a memory that he'd ignored but that suddenly bore consideration.

"That night," he began, watching her face carefully, "the night of the party . . . when everyone was gone and you saw my reflection in the mirror . . . I'd forgotten until this moment how deathly frightened you were."

She was quick to defend herself. "Well, of course I was frightened. I thought I was alone."

"No. It was more than that." He paused, trying to draw back her exact words and capture what it was that had bothered him about her reactions. "I remember now . . . you said, *Patrick it's you*. As if you were relieved because you'd thought I was someone . . . or something else."

"It was late. I was exhausted. I . . . I don't remember how I reacted."

She was clearly uneasy now. He could see it in the tense shifting of her shoulders. In the forced absence of reaction in her eyes.

"And that morning when your furnace acted up. When you came running into the cottage, you looked like the hounds of hell were on your tail."

"Yes, well, *you* try waking up to explosive rumbles and see if you don't quake a little in your size-eleven boots. Call me crazy, but the thought of my house blowing up with me in it has a tendency to make me a little edgy."

"And the light in the attic?" he probed gently,

sensing more and more that there was something amiss, no matter how emphatically she denied it.

"Was a little spooky, okay?" she admitted grumpily. "This is, after all, still a strange house. A big house. I'm still getting used to all its little quirks."

"What kind of quirks?"

She didn't answer.

He decided to help her out. "The kind that makes little girls believe the house is haunted? The kind that makes big girls wonder about the same thing?"

She was quiet for a long moment as she stared without seeing the work in front of her. "If you're a big girl like Cory, yes," she said, choosing her words carefully, "you might be tempted to believe that kind of nonsense."

Her implication was clear. "But a big girl like you— you'd never believe, would you? Even if a gossipy real estate broker named Max Stoner filled your head with stories designed to add romance and mystery to a Victorian relic he'd had trouble unloading."

Her eyes snapped to his. "What stories? Max didn't tell me any stories."

He frowned, wanting to kick himself for adding to her unease instead of lessening it. While he found talk of paranormal phenomena and hauntings for the most part merely entertaining, he'd seen too many "unexplained" happenings in his exploits around the globe to dismiss anything as impossible. It was obvious, however, that Merry was struggling with the notion.

"Old Max must be slipping," he said, attempting to

make light of Max and the stories he evidently didn't tell. "I've always wondered," he began, deciding from the look in her eyes that it was time for a shift of topics, "what it was that compelled you to buy this place, anyway."

She eyed him suspiciously. With a determined jut of her chin she stacked the papers on her lap. Tucking her feet beneath her, she faced him Indian-style from the opposite end of the sofa. "Oh, no, you don't. You started this little foray into the ghastly, ghostly gray area, Patrick. I'd suggest you finish it before you change the subject. What kind of stories does Max tell about this house?"

He set his books aside and gave her his complete attention. It wasn't difficult. A radiant melting took place in his chest as he looked at her.

The feelings she dredged up inside him still amazed him. He wanted to protect her. He wanted to soothe her. And right now, watching the sexy pout of lips still a little swollen from their lovemaking, hair shiny-clean and in need of a thorough mussing from his hands, he wanted to pleasure her. He could placate her later, he decided.

"Oh, no." She shook her head when she recognized the intent behind his wicked grin. "I asked you a question. I want some answers."

"I want some answers too," he said, reaching for her. "Like . . . what are you wearing under that sweater?"

She swatted his hand away. The resistance, he

decided, was token. Her papers spilled to the floor as he reached for her again.

He found his own answers then as he drew her to him so that she straddled his lap. Tunneling his hands up and under her sweater, his broad palms encountered bare breasts, hot and heavy and sweet.

His gaze slid with lazy hunger to hers. He could see in her eyes, beautifully glazed with awakening desire, that the answers she now craved ran in tandem with his.

He eased to his back, settling her feminine weight over his hips, where his arousal lay heavy and hard beneath his fly.

"Take it off," he ordered, never breaking eye contact.

In a slow, sensual motion she crossed her arms in front of her and grasped the hem of the sweater. He watched, his throat constricted, his pulse racing, as she brazenly lifted the sweater up and over her head.

Poised over him like a pagan priestess, she let the sweater slip unheeded from her fingers. Her moist lips glistening, her chestnut hair tousled and untamed, she tempted him with the gentle sway of her breasts, a subtle shifting of her heat against his.

There were words he wanted to say to her. Love words. Lust words. But for once Patrick Ryan was speechless.

From the beginning he'd known she bewitched him, but never more than now. He was starting to realize the extent of her power over him.

The moment he'd kissed her, he'd been lost. The

moment he'd finally made sweet, aching love to her, he'd been found.

And in this moment, as she leaned over him, brushing the velvet-soft tips of her breasts across his waiting mouth, he accepted the truth of what was happening.

For the first time in his life he was falling in love . . . helplessly, unalterably in love . . . with a woman and her promise-me-forever eyes.

EIGHT

Somehow it ended up twilight. Some time ago, they'd made their way back to her bed. And some way, Merry was determined to keep her growing feelings for Patrick in perspective. Chemistry, she kept telling herself. Nothing more.

Stacking her hands on his chest, she propped her chin on top of them and studied the stubble beginning to darken his jaw. Okay, so she liked him. What was not to like? Besides being the most incredible lover she'd ever imagined, he was kind and caring, and he made her laugh. But while liking and loving were certainly fine things, nothing had changed the fact that love was an option she couldn't afford.

"Problem, love?"

She hid her dark thoughts with a staged scowl. "It's your fault I'm going to be working late tomorrow night on the Clayborne account."

"My fault?" he asked, then grunted in understanding. "I take it it's the Clayborne account that's scattered all over the floor in front of the fire?"

"Among other things," she said, then joined him in a grin as she thought of the clothes that were also tossed about the drawing-room floor.

"Guess I'll have to think of a way to make it up to you." His eyes, though sleepy with satisfaction, danced as he nudged her with his hips.

She snorted softly. "There's a word for men like you."

"Extraordinary?" he suggested hopefully.

"Randy."

He grinned and nudged her again. "That too."

She rolled her eyes. "Not that the idea doesn't have its appeal, but I had something else in mind."

He ran his hands in a lazy caress down the length of her back. "Name it."

She hesitated, wondering if she really wanted to broach the subject. In the end her curiosity won the argument. "I was hoping you'd supply some answers."

"Answers?"

"Before you distracted me," she began, hoping she sounded more relaxed than she felt, "I believe you were about to tell me the stories Max Stoner never got around to sharing."

"Oh, that."

"Yeah, that."

He cupped her bottom in both hands and gave her a light squeeze. "Up with you, then. If I've got to sing, it's going to be for my supper. I don't know about you, but I'm starved. And I have my reputation to think of."

"Reputation?"

"It's that stamina you're so impressed with. While I'd like to think I could, this is one man who does not live on love alone."

She squirmed suggestively against him. "You sure you don't want to put it to the test?"

He laughed and hugged her tight. "Have mercy on me, Merry. The heart is willing, but the body . . ."

"The body needs nourishment," she finished for him. Nipping him lightly on the chin, she slipped out of bed. "Come on. Let's see what we can do to stave off malnutrition and put the starch back in your . . . ah . . ."

"My ah what?" he asked, grinning broadly.

"Well, it certainly isn't your attitude," she said with a cheeky smile.

While Merry straightened up the living room, Patrick found a couple of apples, some cheese, some pâté, and a bottle of chilled wine. He set everything on the table with an assortment of crackers.

"Sit," he ordered when Merry joined him in the kitchen. "Eat." Dropping a kiss on her forehead, he settled her in a chair.

"Sit. Talk," she countered meaningfully, and held out her wineglass for him to fill.

"What do you want to know?"

"You hinted that Max told certain stories."

"Max has always had a flair for drama."

"And . . . ?"

"And he was fond of romancing the past of the old relic. No disrespect intended," he added hastily, "but you've got to admit, the old girl has seen better days. Which leads me back to my question: Why *did* you buy this place, Merry? It's not exactly the stuff dreams are made of."

The stuff dreams are made of. She would have laughed at his choice of words had they not hit so close to home. Until she started having the dreams, she hadn't even entertained the notion of buying a house. Until the dreams and the house and Patrick her life had been pretty . . . lifeless, she admitted reluctantly.

"It was someone's dream once." Her heartfelt statement surprised her. Then she fell back on her old stand-by. "Besides, it was a good buy."

"That's because Max was having trouble unloading it."

"Why?"

"You mean besides the obvious reasons that it needs major renovations, is a high-maintenance property, and is ugly as sin?"

"It's not ugly. It's beautiful—at least it's becoming beautiful again. Why else was he having trouble selling it?"

"Maybe hinting to prospective buyers that the house might be haunted had something to do with it."

She hid her concern by spreading pâté on a cracker and handing it to him. "Max did that?"

He nodded, stuffed the cracker into his mouth, and talked around it. "As I said, he seemed to think it added to the romance. But the stories backfired. Instead of adding intrigue, the haunted-house business made people a little edgy. They began to believe it. And who's to say?" He cast a nervous but completely staged glance over his shoulder. "Maybe it *is* haunted."

"That's ridiculous," she said, a bit too quickly.

Frowning, he shrugged. "Maybe."

She studied him while he loaded a cracker and offered it to her. "What was Max's ghost supposed to have done to attract so much attention?"

He cocked his head back and squinted thoughtfully at the ceiling. "I don't know if there was anything specific . . . more like a hovering presence. A lonely spirit, Max used to say, who just wandered around as if it were looking for something, or someone. Fairly passive, as ghosts go."

She thought of the creaking floors and unexplained lights and shivered. "It sounds as if Max has an overactive imagination."

"And what about your imagination? Is it a bit active too? Is that the real reason Cory brought you the books?"

"I explained that," she said, hoping he wouldn't probe further. "What about you? You've rented the cottage for what? Ten years now? Have you ever thought there was anything strange going on over here?"

Again he shrugged, considering. "Only the turnover. Max would just get the place rented with an option to buy, and six months later they'd be gone and the deal would be off. Since I was gone so much of the time, I can't tell you why every potential buyer seemed to find a reason to leave. And then, until you came along, the house sat empty for the last couple of years."

She sipped her wine, aware of his considering silence.

"Is there a reason for these questions, Merry? Other than curiosity, I mean. Is there something going on over here you're not telling me about?"

"No." She drew a bracing breath, then smiled. "I'm just curious . . . about the house. About its history."

"You're not a believer, then?" he asked when she fidgeted under his stare.

"A believer?"

"In ghosts. In the possibility that souls from past lives can make connections with souls in the present."

His eyes grew very dark as he watched her. So dark, it made her wonder what thoughts were hidden behind his benign look.

"Do you believe?" she asked in a voice made small by apprehension.

"Believe? Yeah." He drained his glass and smiled at her. "I believe. I believe we've exhausted this conversation, and it's time to move on to bigger and better things."

She recognized his intent and grinned in spite of herself. "Such as?"

"Such as that willing heart of mine." He reached for her and drew her onto his lap. "It's managed to coax my body into going along with it."

Looping her arms over his shoulders, she leaned into his kiss. "Well, bless that little Irish heart."

"And?" he murmured, pressing the ridged strength of his arousal against her hip.

"And every other Irish part."

Chuckling, he rose and carried her back to bed.

Monday morning Merry marched into the office and unceremoniously dumped the entire armload of books onto Cory's desk.

Cory glanced from the books to Merry, an expectant light brightening her eyes. "Well?"

Merry shrugged out of her coat and hung it on the rack behind the door. "Well, what?"

"Well, did you discover anything interesting from the books?"

"As a matter of fact, I did," Merry answered thoughtfully.

"I knew it! I knew they'd give you some answers. So tell me. What'd you find out?"

Merry settled in behind her desk. "To get rid of a toothache, try spitting into a frog's mouth, kissing a donkey, or strangling a mole. Other than that, nothing else seemed too pertinent."

Deflated, Cory scowled at her. "You didn't read them, did you?"

"No, I didn't read them. I'm not *going* to read them. And I don't want to hear about what *you* read in them. End of discussion."

After her question-and-answer period with Patrick, Merry had made up her mind to forget this ghost business once and for all. She wasn't about to let a gossipy broker's tall tales shake her faith in fact over fiction.

Cory slumped back in her chair. "You're no fun, Mer."

"Yeah, well, come up with a different game, and we'll see if I can play it with a little more enthusiasm."

While Merry sensed from the way Cory was thumbing through the books that she hadn't spoken her last word on the subject, she did, for the time being at least, drop it.

"Speaking of games . . ." A suggestive smile tilted Cory's lips. "Did you and Patrick indulge in any, ah, special activities this weekend after Jerry and I left?"

One particularly special activity they'd indulged in came vividly to Merry's mind. Late Sunday afternoon Patrick had coaxed her into a romp in her bathtub that had added new dimension to the time-honored tradition of bobbing for apples. She smiled, then checked it when she felt color flood her cheeks.

"Yeah." Recognizing that look, Cory sighed dreamily. "Me too. Ain't love grand?"

Merry shot her a warning glare. "Love, Cory? Jerry's a sweetheart, but you just met him."

"Well, you just met Patrick," Cory fired back defensively.

"*You're* the one talking about love," Merry insisted, trying to regain her no-nonsense persona for Cory's benefit.

"And you're not?" Cory snorted. "I was born at night, Mer, but it wasn't *last* night. Any fool can see you're crazy about him."

"I am not *crazy* about him," she insisted, fidgeting in her chair.

"And he's nuts over you."

"Why do I get the feeling we're going to go home tonight and write in our diaries?" Merry grumbled. "Anyone eavesdropping on this conversation would think we were a couple of bubble-gummers high on our first crush, not two mature women—" She glanced up just as Cory stuck her tongue out at her. "Make that *one* mature woman trying to keep things in perspective."

"Mature women face their problems and try to solve them. They don't bury their heads in the Sahara and wait for them to go away."

"And what's that supposed to mean?"

"You said you didn't want to talk about it."

"That," Merry said pointedly, knowing Cory was referring to the dreams and the excess baggage that came with them, "is not a problem. It's a coincidence."

Cory looked at her sharply. "If it's not a problem,

then why can't you talk about it? And why did you lie to Patrick about the key?"

Merry glanced up guiltily, then away. "Let's just get to work, okay?"

Cory frowned, then gave her a gentle smile of understanding before digging into the listings on her desk.

Between a hectic schedule at Collectibles and a wealth of attention from Patrick, Merry's week flew by in a whirl of falling leaves and cooling temperatures. When time permitted and Patrick wasn't with her, she turned the house upside down looking, in vain, for the missing key.

She'd come to realize that taking Patrick to her bed had also turned her life upside down. She now viewed it as a major mistake—but one she couldn't bring herself to correct. Knowing it was wrong, she let work fill her days . . . and Patrick fill her nights.

On one of those nights, as she lay awake in a puddle of moonlight and Patrick's arms, she considered telling him about the dreams. In the afterglow of his loving, in the suspended grace of sated pleasure, anything seemed possible. That was because everything about Patrick was easy: coming home each day to find him waiting for her; accepting the unspoken agreement that they would share the nights in her bed.

As he stirred in his sleep and drew her closer, his possessive gesture filled her heart with tenderness. She wanted nothing more than to nestle deeper into his heat and absorb the solid, substantial beat of his heart pounding steadily against hers.

It was then that the truth hit her. She couldn't tell him about the dreams or about the key—or about any of her problems. She could do nothing that would increase their emotional intimacy, because of the very real threat of her falling in love with him.

She couldn't let love happen. He could hurt her, just as Gavin had—only this time she might not recover.

She'd realized how great her danger was the night in her kitchen when he'd told her about the adventures that served as the basis for his writing. She'd seen it in Patrick's eyes—the drive to be different, to live on the edge. The wanderlust she envied but didn't understand.

Gavin had had it too. He'd never been content with what he had within reach; he'd always wanted more. When he'd come to her asking for a divorce because life—specifically life as it related to their marriage—had lost its spark, she'd almost been expecting it. But she'd been unprepared for the pain, the devastating loss of self-esteem.

She couldn't go through it again. And she wouldn't if she just kept her head. This time she was prepared. She'd known from the beginning that permanency wasn't an option with Patrick.

I've known a lot of women, he'd told her. *I don't possess the staying power for anything long-term*. Though his warnings had been gentle, he hadn't minced words. Each one was indelibly etched in her mind. She repeated them daily like a mantra.

So she wouldn't tell him about the dreams because in a sense, confiding in him would constitute a far greater intimacy than the physical intimacy they shared. For her own protection she would keep that part of herself distant.

Besides, the dreams had ended the night she'd taken Patrick to her bed. For her own peace of mind she'd decided not to question why.

Just as she'd decided not to love Patrick.

Sensing a subtle change in his breathing beside her, she turned her head on the pillow. He was awake, and watching her.

"Are you thinking of him, then?" he asked in a gruff whisper. "Your husband, love," he added when her brows furrowed.

She looked away, uncomfortable with his ability to read her thoughts.

He expelled a heavy breath. "Is that why you look so troubled sometimes?" Tucking her snugly against him, he murmured into her hair, "Do you still love him, Merry?"

She stared into the darkness, wondering at the uncertainty of his tone. "It's not a question of love. Not anymore."

"But thinking of him still hurts you."

"Yes," she answered truthfully. "It hurts some-

imes. But we all need reminders of past hurts to keep
hem from happening again."

A long silence crowded into the room, competing
with the darkness and the moonglow. "And what was it
hat hurt you so badly you won't let it happen again?"

She turned to him. Something far deeper than
concern carved soft shadows on his face.

"Love," she said, looking quickly away, not daring
o believe that the very emotion she was denying had
darkened his eyes and softened his voice. "Love happened."

"And now you're afraid?"

Yes, she was afraid, but she wouldn't let him know
t. "Now I'm wise."

"Merry—"

"Shhh." She pressed trembling fingers to his lips.
'Please . . . don't say things that are better left unsaid. What we have is good. And if we leave it at this,
hen we won't ever hurt or disappoint each other."

After a long, searching look she turned away from
him, purposefully erecting an emotional distance much
farther than the six inches of cold sheets between them.

And then she pretended to sleep, pretended she
wasn't already in love with him, pretended she wasn't
painfully aware of his brooding, wakeful silence well
nto the night.

Patrick's writing had been going well. At least it had
been until last night, when Merry had made her midnight declaration that she'd sworn off love.

Giving up the hope of producing any salvageable material, he flipped the switch on his word processor, laced his hands behind his head, leaned back in his chair, and considered what he was going to do to change her mind. He didn't even question when he'd become so set on changing it. He knew he should be feeling relief that she had no intention of falling in love again. A week ago he would have. A week ago he wasn't in love himself.

Since he was relatively inexperienced in the emotion, he had to believe that the experts on the subject were right: Love conquers all.

They'd better be right, because the prospect of losing Merry was unthinkable. It made him feel weak as he'd never felt weak before. The same man who had in the course of his career scaled unscalable mountains, infiltrated guerrilla encampments in Central America, played the equivalent of Russian roulette with a renegade CIA agent, was suddenly shaking in his boots at the thought of losing one soft, fragile woman.

Well, even before Merry, he'd realized he was getting a bit tired of that life. . . . For one thing, he was getting too old for it. For another, money, the great motivator, was no longer in short supply.

He glanced at the books lined up on his desk . . . all ten his, the last seven best-sellers, all responsible for his current level of success.

He knew he had to tell her he wasn't the starving artist she was content to think he was. To that end, he'd offered to let her read some of his work. She hadn't really refused. She'd just made a vague excuse about not having the time right now . . . that she'd be sure to make time soon.

He knew her game, though. She didn't want to read his books because by doing so, she would get to know him better. She wanted to keep an emotional distance.

He was determined to bridge that distance. He just hadn't figured out how. She did that to him: made him question, made him doubt.

He was unaccustomed to feeling vulnerable. He did not wear vulnerability well. Didn't like the fabric, didn't like the fit.

He swore silently. How he longed to just march over there and take her by storm, instead of biding his time like a schoolboy afraid to ask for his first date.

It ought to be easier than this. After all, he'd waited thirty-eight years to find her. She was the only woman he'd ever truly loved. And he'd be damned if he'd let her blow off the notion because some other bastard had hurt her so badly, she was afraid to try it again.

He could not lose her. Yet he realized that he would if he didn't play this just right.

He walked to the kitchen, dug into the fridge, and flipped the top on a beer. Staring at the descent of evening, he decided that what she needed was time. And attention. He could provide both. And while time went about healing her wounds, he'd go about winning her heart.

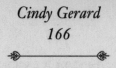

The kitten was as soft as down and as black as a witch's hat. Cradling the mewing ball of fur to her breast, Merry stood in her open doorway and looked around for a clue as to how the basket, and its precious cargo, had ended up on her front porch.

A deep voice, rich with traces of an Irish brogue, wished her "Happy Halloween" from the shadows.

The heart she'd been trying so hard to guard melted a little more.

"I should have known," she said, slipping outside.

Joining her under the porch light, Patrick touched a large finger to the kitten's small head. "To warm your feet at night."

Her eyes sought his, but she hid the tenderness she felt for him with a teasing grin. "I thought I had you for that."

He grinned engagingly. "Would be a waste of my talents, love. I'll hold out for the more intricate duties."

"Duties?" she said, arching a brow.

"Well, certain duties do have their perks."

Apparently satisfied that he'd made her blush, he glanced down at the kitten. "What do you think? Is he a keeper?"

Cuddling the squirming kitten to her cheek, she met Patrick's eyes again, aware that hers had misted over with a tender emotion she fought against identifying or naming. "I think you both are."

Damn the man. It had been two weeks since she'd found him watching her in the night. Hadn't he listened when she'd told him she wasn't about to let herself fall in love again? Didn't he know that every time he did or said something sweet, he chipped another piece out of that barrier she wanted so badly to keep intact?

Didn't he know that he was setting her up for a fall?

Battling back the tears that threatened to swamp her, she motioned with her head toward the door. "Come on. Let's see what he thinks of his new home."

Patrick closed the door behind them, shutting out the crisp October chill. "What are you going to name him?"

"I don't know." She considered the kitten as she set it on the floor, then grinned as it tested the polished parquet floor for traction. "I guess I'll have to get to know him a bit better before I decide what fits him."

Catching her around her waist, Patrick gathered her against him. "Sound reasoning. After all, it worked for me. Until I got to know you better, I'd never have guessed that you were such a wild little wanton."

She looped her arms around his neck, determined not to let him wangle another blush out of her. "You've only yourself to blame for finding that particular flaw in my character."

"Flaw? Merry, Merry. There's where you're wrong. Flaw*less* is what I think of when I think of you. And I think of you . . . often." He nudged her with his hips. "As a matter of fact, if you knew what I was thinking at this moment, you'd—"

"I think"—she grinned, finding it easier to play with him than be angry with him—"that some thoughts are better left unsaid. Especially now. We're about to be set upon by a horde of goblins and ghosts."

"So put the candy outside the door and let the little beggars fend for themselves."

"Patrick, you're awful."

His eyes twinkled. "And you love it."

The doorbell rang.

Moving away from her with a grin, he picked up the bowl of candy she'd purchased for the night's events. "I'll get rid of them."

"You'll do no such thing." Laughing, she snatched the bowl out of his hand and opened the door to a set of miniatures—a clown, a pirate, and a Ninja Turtle. Patrick, she noted with a smile, was right beside her, clearly enjoying the pint-sized trick-or-treaters despite his grousing.

"Trick or treat!" the crew chorused in unison.

The stream of characters and creatures was fairly steady until eight o'clock and delighted both of them. After an hour of silence they assumed that the little monsters and superheroes were probably home bouncing off their parents' walls from an overload of sugar.

So when the doorbell rang at 9:00 P.M., it was with sleepy surprise that Merry roused herself from a crackling fire and Patrick's arms. Settling the kitten in his lap, she left him on the sofa, assuring him she could handle this latecomer by herself.

Candy bowl in hand, she opened the door. But her front porch was empty.

She frowned. Shading her eyes against the glare from the porch light, she squinted into the night. A lone dark figure hurried down the walk toward the curb.

Merry's first reaction was that some mother ought to be horse-whipped for letting her little boy or girl out alone so late and in clothes so dark the driver of a passing car would never see the child. Her second thought was that the black-draped goblin was awfully big for a child.

"Don't be shy." She stepped out onto the porch. "We've still got treats left for you."

She descended the steps to the sidewalk, uncomfortably aware of a stark, unnatural stillness, a stale, clammy heaviness that had settled in the air.

She stopped. The goblin stopped. And waited.

"*Merry* . . ."

Her name seemed to ride on the currents of the night. Softly spoken . . . from a distance . . . the sound an eerie intrusion of earthy longing and unearthly agony.

Mesmerized, she stared at the figure that, impossible as it seemed, appeared to blend into the drifting shadows.

She took a hesitant step forward. Then another. No moonlight illuminated her path as she made her way carefully into the darkness. Clouds had gathered and brought an icy chill to the crisp October night.

A shiver rippled through her as she searched beyond the shadows.

"Who are you?" she asked, her heart suddenly pounding like thunder.

The apparition turned to face her, a huddle of black rags exuding a chilling sense of loneliness, faceless beneath the folds of a draping hood.

"Who are you?" she whispered again. "Cory, if that's you, I swear you'll pay for this."

A long-fingered hand, bound in dripping scraps of black gauze, reached with great effort to tug back the hood. Just as the hood started sliding away from the face, a gust of wind swirled around Merry's ankles. Icy cold, fierce with power, it kicked up fallen leaves and dust in such a flurry, she covered her face with her arm. Then, just as suddenly as it had come, the mysterious wind was gone.

She lowered her arm, raked her hair away from her eyes . . . and found herself alone.

"Merry?"

She jumped, then pressed a hand to her heart when Patrick walked up beside her.

"What are you doing out here, love? You'll catch your death."

Numb, shaken by what she had—or hadn't—seen, she smiled tremulously up at him.

"Must have been a trickster," she mumbled weakly.

He frowned down at her, tucked her under his shoulder, and steered her back to the house. "Goes with the holiday."

"Right. With the holiday," she said softly. Yet for the first time in her life, she seriously considered the possible existence of ghosts and goblins and things that went bump in the night.

NINE

Merry named the kitten Mystery, because after a week she'd decided that's exactly what he was. One minute he'd be underfoot arching and rubbing against her legs; the next minute he'd be gone. Vanished. Until he was hungry or wanted some attention, or a warm, soft place to curl up and take a nap.

That warm, soft place quite often turned out to be Patrick's lap, or the curve behind Merry's knees in the middle of the night, provided Patrick wasn't occupying that spot himself. Which he often was.

After a week in Mystery's company Merry couldn't imagine a life without him. After a month with Patrick she found herself thinking the same thing. It was the latter thought that presented her most persistent dilemma.

Owning up to and dealing with her increasingly deeper emotional involvement with Patrick, however, was not her immediate problem. Mystery was.

"Here kitty, kitty, kitty. Here, Mystery. I hear you, baby, but where are you?"

It was late Sunday afternoon. Patrick had taken off earlier to run some errands. Merry had been searching the first floor for Mystery for the better part of an hour. She could hear his occasional cry but hadn't been able to pinpoint his location.

The cry didn't sound particularly fretful. It was just persistent. She was beginning to worry that the kitten might be trapped somewhere.

Exhausting every nook and cubbyhole on the first floor, she climbed the stairs to the second. The mewing grew louder.

"Come on, kitty. Come here, Mystery."

Her call was met by silence. She'd started toward her bedroom and was wondering if she might have accidentally shut him in the closet when she heard him again.

She stopped, listened, and decided the meows were coming from above her. Which could mean only one thing: Mystery was somewhere on the third floor near the attic door.

She drew a deep breath and walked toward the upper level's landing.

"This is so stupid," she muttered when she realized her legs were a little shaky and her heart was pumping a beat or two faster than normal. She'd avoided the attic like the plague. Because of the light? Yes. She admitted that was the reason, even though she'd blamed it on the locked door and the missing key.

How had Cory put it? *The bats and the bogeymen can take the third floor.* Well, she'd left the attic to those unknowns, and in the process had added credence to the possibility of their existence.

Not exactly a font of rational thought these days, are you, Merry? she mused in disgust. She had to admit, Cory's preoccupation with paranormal phenomena had gotten to her. So had the episode Halloween Eve; a chill coiled up her spine whenever she thought of her mysterious visitor. And she thought of it often.

Had her goblin been real? Or had she just imagined it?

The kitten meowed again. Merry snapped her head toward the sound, walked to the landing, and peered up into the shadows.

"Kitty?"

Silence.

Drawing a bracing breath, she squared her shoulders and began to climb the stairs.

The windowless hallway was narrow and dark, the wallpaper age-stained and faded. The scent of dust, old plaster, and must closed in on her like a warning. This arena was not of her time. Not of her place. Ignoring her growing sense of unease and foreboding, she climbed the last step and faced the attic door.

"Kitty?"

Something snaked like smoke around her ankle. She gasped, gripping the old brass doorknob for support. Just as swiftly as it came, the feeling drifted away.

It could have been a draft, she told herself, willing her hammering heart to settle down.

"Meow."

It could have been Mystery.

She slumped in relief as the kitten's downy-soft tail brushed against her ankle again, a gesture of welcome, a playful hello.

"Mystery." She sighed and knelt to pick him up and cuddle him to her cheek. "You little demon. I was worried about you. And you managed to scare me half to death," she added in a self-censuring sputter.

The kitten's purr thrummed against her cheek, a steady little motor that felt substantial and warm and eased the chilling thoughts of a moment ago.

She stroked his back. "What are you doing up here, anyway?"

Mystery squirmed free and jumped to the floor.

Merry's eyes had finally adjusted to the dim light. She watched the kitten as it arched and curled its tail, pacing back and forth on tiptoes in front of the attic door.

"You want in there, do you? Think maybe there's a mouse or two to torment? Sorry, baby, but without a key—"

She stopped abruptly when something caught her eye. Something metallic and dull that was wedged between the faded wallpaper and the baseboard by the kitten's fuzzy tail.

With an unsteady hand she reached for it and tugged it free.

She stared at the key in her hand, then shook her head in denial. She swore it hadn't been here when she'd looked for it both before and after Patrick had told her about the light in the attic. And she *had* looked. One of the first places she'd searched had been on the floor near the door.

It was here now. In her hand. Cold and heavy. An invitation. A dare.

Mystery mewed again and scratched at the door. Taking a deep breath, Merry reminded herself that the threat of the unknown was always stronger than the known.

She slipped the key in the lock.

The latch was stiff. Like old, arthritic bones, the hinges sang a creaky complaint as she shoved the door open.

The kitten scampered into the attic room.

"Mystery, come back!" she called as the kitten disappeared into a dark corner.

Hesitant, Merry stood in the middle of the open doorway. She looked slowly around her. *There*, she mused silently. *See? It's not so scary. It's just a dark, empty old attic with a maze of cobwebs clinging to electric wires and bare rafters*. A single light bulb hung from a spindly wire in the middle of the room.

"Come on, Mystery." She rubbed her arms to ward off the chill of the drafty room. "Let's go back downstairs where it's warm and not so dusty. Mystery?" she called again and stepped into the room, making a visual search of the corners.

"There you are, you little devil." Spotting him chasing a dust ball along the floor near a sloping wall, she bent down to scoop him up.

At the same moment she stood, the sun broke through a heavy layer of wind clouds. Sunlight streamed through a high dormer window, cutting through the haze to cast a cylindrical tunnel of light on the far corner of the attic. It spilled like a muzzy spotlight on an old oak chest sitting there.

She frowned. When Max had given her the grand tour, the attic had been empty.

The sun tucked behind the clouds again. The dark oak and aged leather of the chest blended back into the shadows once more.

Intrigued, compelled, Merry reached for the pull string on the light and tugged it on. The single bulb barely brightened the room, but it was enough. She walked slowly across the bare wood floor. Setting the kitten down beside her, she knelt in front of the chest.

Anticipation, curiosity, and a humming sense of discovery filled her as she carefully lifted the lid.

The telling scent of time enfolded her as her gaze swept in silent wonder over the chest's contents. Heavy woolen trousers and age-yellowed linen shirts met her eye. A pair of suspenders. A favorite book.

A packet of letters bound with a pale pink ribbon.

In a fog Merry reached for the packet. Careful of the fragile parchment, struggling with her trembling fingers, she slipped the top sheet free.

Her heart knew before she did. It began a hard, heavy beat even before she unfolded the first faintly leather-scented sheet and began to read.

My beloved Jamie, the letter began. . . .

Patrick found her in the attic, on her knees before a chest on the floor. Sunlight flowed like a golden curtain around her, caught on the crystal stream of tears that tracked down her face and spilled to the papers in her lap.

"Merry?"

She looked up at him, her eyes filled with a poignant sadness. And something else. Something that mystified and mesmerized him and played havoc with the beat of his heart.

"Love . . . what is it?"

She looked so small sitting there. So fragile. And never more beautiful as she held out a trembling hand, a silent plea to join her.

Clasping her hand in both of his, he dropped to his knees beside her. One touch and he physically felt the need in her. The need for reality, for flesh and blood, for earth and earthiness.

"What is it?" he repeated, anxious for her now.

For the rest of his life he would remember the look in her eyes. It was a haunted look, a plaintive plea that was transformed in a pulse beat to a desperate wanting. The force of it staggered him.

I need you, her eyes pleaded. *And I need you not to question why*.

It wasn't a request; it was an ardent command, a stunning surrender to emotions he couldn't begin to comprehend. He didn't know what had happened to her up here in the attic. He understood only the strength of her solitary experience. The power. The undeniable urgency that had claimed her . . . and was now claiming him as well.

He reached for her, drawing her against him. She melted into his embrace, all restless wanting and raging desire.

Their mouths met in a wild clash of seeking tongues and hungry, wet heat. She bit his lip with a savagery that excited and enflamed him and fed the fire within to a licking blaze.

Without breaking the kiss, he wrenched off his leather jacket. Tossing it to the floor, he laid her back on the supple leather and knelt over her.

"Hurry," she pleaded, as he tore off his shirt and unbuttoned his fly.

She reached for him, claiming his arousal with questing hands, uninhibited yearning. With a groan he stripped off her jeans and panties.

"Now. Please," she cried, then gasped when he parted her thighs and thrust deep inside her. So deep, he thought he'd hurt her. So hard, he thought he'd died in an agony of pleasure.

Back arched, he lowered his head to her breasts and suckled her greedily through her blouse. It wasn't enough. With a fierce disregard for buttons and patience, he ripped the blouse open and flicked the clasp of her bra.

Bending to her again, he drew her deeply into his mouth. She moaned low in her throat. He craved that small sound of triumphant surrender as much as he craved the honeyed taste of her, the generous weight of her filling his mouth, the tight, sweet heat of her body clenching around him as he pumped into her again and again.

Heat and heaven crashed together in a blinding rush of sensation. Gripping her hips in his hands, he thrust deep as a huge, convulsive shudder rippled through his body. She cried out as she climaxed. Then, murmuring her name through clenched teeth, he too surrendered to the passion, to a physical and emotional release more vital and demanding than any mere act of love could have provided.

It struck him then that they hadn't just made love. They'd made magic. And as he held her compliant body against his and looked into her eyes, he felt consumed by the notion that they had just made history.

He was a long time coming down. A long time in awe of this woman. He feathered a kiss across her brow. When she stirred, he whispered another kiss to her hair.

Beneath his elbows the floor was growing hard and

cold. Beneath his body hers had begun to tremble. A chilling draft drifted across the faint sheen of perspiration covering his back. If he could have moved, he would have. As it was, he could hardly think, barely breathe. He still filled her, yet he felt achingly full of her.

With her hair tangled around his fingers, her clothes crumpled and torn, her golden limbs twined with his in an exhausted sprawl, she looked the wild, reckless lover. Yet the pallor beneath her flushed cheeks, the shallow breaths she drew, reminded him how fragile and shaken he'd found her.

He pressed another kiss to her temple, where her pulse still fluttered in the aftermath of their urgent joining. "Are you all right, love?"

She was slow to open her eyes. When she did, the mellow glow of latent passion was colored by a distant distress.

His heart lurched. "Oh, God. I've hurt you."

"No," she assured him quickly. She closed her eyes and tried to pull herself together. She didn't quite manage it. "Patrick . . . we have to talk."

He searched her face, gauging her need and the depth of the trouble darkening her eyes. "Yes," he said, a creeping unease diminishing the wonder they'd just shared, "it seems as if we do."

He refused to let her talk until he'd drawn a hot tub to warm her, wrapped her in his own heavy robe, and settled her in front of the fire with a cup of hot chocolate.

Even then, even after the delay, she hesitated. Finally, haltingly, staring alternately at the fire and the cup in her hands but never at him, she told him. Everything.

He didn't know what he'd been expecting her to say. That she loved him, maybe. That she didn't love him. Nothing would have surprised him—nothing but what she actually told him.

He rose from the sofa and raked his hand through his hair. His mind raced to absorb her story. The book of poetry, the inscription, the dreams, her impulsive purchase of the house. No wonder she'd looked so frightened that night she'd seen him in the mirror. She'd thought he was this Jamie character. And then there was the light in the attic. The mysterious disappearing goblin. The talk of hauntings and the reality of clanging furnaces and disappearing keys.

"Why didn't you tell me about this before?"

"How?" A look of helpless defeat crossed her face. "Just announce over bagels, 'Oh, by the way, did I happen to mention that I dreamed about you before I ever met you? That you made love to me in those dreams on a nightly basis before I even knew your name?'" Her eyes took on a dull sheen of desperation. "I didn't want to believe it myself. How could I expect you to?"

He watched her quietly. "What about now? Do you believe it now?"

She let her head drop wearily against the sofa. "I don't know." She stared at the ceiling, then at him. "I don't know what to believe. I . . . just know I can't deny what's happening any longer."

He wanted to be angry with her for keeping this from him. He wasn't so sure that he wasn't. He was sure of only one thing: He was overwhelmed by his own unwillingness to believe what she was telling him.

"Why today, Merry? Why did it take you until today to tell me?"

She sighed heavily. "The letters."

"Letters?"

"I found Merry's letters. In the chest."

He glanced toward the attic. "I'll be right back."

He took the stairs two at a time. When he came back with the hastily gathered stack of letters, Mystery was curled up on Merry's lap. She stroked the kitten absently as she stared into the fire.

In all, there were a dozen letters. All of them began, *My beloved Jamie*. All of them ended, *When are you going to send for me?* All were signed, *I'll wait forever, Merry Clare*.

Each letter was a poignantly moving declaration of young love. And each was more urgent than the last, each more filled with a sense of lost love, a painful awareness that Jamie's plans to send for Merry must have gone awry.

When Patrick looked up from the last one, Merry was watching him.

"I feel her pain." Her words and the emotion behind them spilled out with simple, awful candor. Tears glistened as she repeated with the same sense of helplessness, the same bleak despair that infused each letter, "I feel her pain."

Patrick wrapped her gently in his arms, knowing instinctively what she was thinking. "I'm not Jamie," he said softly. "And I'm not Gavin. I'm here. And I'm not going to leave you."

Though she settled without resistance against him, her tone was hushed, her words laced with weary acceptance. "Yes," she said. "Yes, you will."

He knew of only one way to reassure her. He took her to bed and loved her until she slept.

And then the very next day he did exactly what he'd promised he wouldn't do. He left her.

Patrick called her at the office to tell her he was leaving. Though she'd been anticipating this moment from the beginning, it stunned her just the same.

Gripping the phone with both hands, she squeezed her eyes shut and listened. Fragmented pieces of his hurried explanation blended into a fog of disappointment and pain. He couldn't talk. He had a plane to catch. An unexpected call from his agent. Two days—three max. He was sorry. He'd be back.

Only one part of his message came through loud and clear. He was leaving.

By Wednesday evening the shock had worn off . . . and the hurting she'd been trying to deny had started again in earnest. She missed him. Missed him the way a bird would miss the wind.

Waiting beside the microwave for a cup of soup to heat, Merry stared tiredly out the kitchen window. Patrick's cottage was as dark as the night. She dragged her gaze back to the microwave and watched the seconds tick off. Long after the buzzer sounded, she stood there. Listening to the sound that was only silence. The emptiness that was her life.

Forcing herself to move, she carried the mug to the table and managed to swallow a spoonful. It was all she got down before a deep ache gripped her.

She'd expected him to leave, hadn't she? She just hadn't wanted to hurt his badly when he actually left.

Maybe if she hadn't told him about the dreams. The look on his face as he'd listened had been one of shock. Shock and wary compassion. And disbelief.

She didn't blame him for his reaction. In fact, she'd felt sympathy for him. Her story had made him uncomfortable. Though his questions had been gentle, even sincere, she'd known what he was thinking. What else could he think? She laughed harshly. Even *she* thought she was crazy.

She stared at her mug of soup. Mystery meowed, reminding her that he, at least, was hungry. Setting out a saucer of milk, she sank down on the floor beside him.

"You miss him, baby?"

Mystery lapped his milk.

"Yeah. Me too."

When the kitten had finished his supper, she cuddled him to her breast, turned out the lights, and climbed the stairs to a bed that had never seemed empty until Patrick had slept in it.

It was half past midnight when Patrick let himself quietly into Merry's kitchen. He was tired, and he was cranky. A contract problem had forced him to fly to New York and kept him there longer than he'd intended. A multitude of problems on his return flight had landed him at the airport a full five hours after his scheduled arrival time. What the hell thunderstorms in Ohio had to do with him catching a plane out of Kennedy he'd never know, but that was the only excuse he'd been given.

He shrugged out of his jacket and flipped the light on over the sink. The first thing he noted was the full cup of soup sitting on the kitchen table. He frowned, then spotted Mystery sidling around the doorway. Blatantly ignoring Patrick, the kitten tippy-toed across the hardwood floor, then stopped and began leisurely washing his face.

"Hello to you too," Patrick whispered, grinning. "Got your nose out of joint because I left, do you?"

Mystery rose and, with regal disregard for Patrick's presence, walked back out of the kitchen.

"Let's hope the mistress of the house is happier to see me," Patrick muttered, and headed for the stairs.

Merry shifted restlessly under the covers. Her mind was playing tricks again. Cruel, delicious tricks that resurrected her wants, magnified her needs.

He was back. In her dreams he was back. Solid strength, musky male heat pressing against her body. A deep Irish brogue whispering a husky caress against her ear.

"Lord, love . . . you'll never know how much I missed you."

She opened her eyes slowly. Shadowed and dark, he bent over her. Daring, elusive. Seductive. Addictive. Her dream lover, with his poet's eyes and lover's mouth that smiled and teased and promised untold pleasures, was back. And she wanted him. She would always want him.

She couldn't help herself. She touched a hand to his midnight-black hair as his nimble fingers undid the buttons on her nightshirt.

"This isn't real," she whispered. A statement. A

denial. A bid to hang on to her sanity. A plea to stay lost in his touch.

He smiled against her breasts. "Ah, but it is. Wake up, love. I don't want you to miss a moment of what I have in mind for you."

The heat of his mouth on her bare skin stole her faltering presence of mind.

"Patrick?" A question. A hope.

"No one else." He kissed her, hard and deep. "There will never be anyone else."

Merry's bed was empty when she woke up in the morning. Patrick's scent on her sheets, however, assured her she hadn't been dreaming. He was back. But for how long?

Grim-faced, she showered, got ready for work, and went downstairs. Hesitating at the kitchen door, she stood for a moment and smelled the coffee, listening to the rustle of a newspaper that told her he was still here. A rush of glad relief filled her.

So this is what she'd come to. Hoping to find him here. Afraid to find him gone.

Shame and defeat pitted against gladness as she pushed through the door. He smiled a mellow "hello" smile over the top of the newspaper. "Good morning."

Another morning she'd have gone to him. Not this one. "Good morning."

Frowning in reaction to the edge in her voice, he slowly folded up the paper. He watched her in silence.

Avoiding his eyes, she poured herself a cup of coffee.

"You're angry, then," he said into the charged silence. "Angry that I left on such short notice."

Angry? Yes. She was angry. But not with him. It wasn't his fault she'd fallen in love with him.

She was desperately happy that he was back—and tormented by that desperation. She'd missed him so much. And the next time he left . . . she'd go through it all over again.

Hating herself for her weakness, she set her cup on the counter. "I'm not angry with you, Patrick."

"Hurt then."

Like an open wound. She checked her watch. "Look . . . I'm sorry. I have to go to work."

He snagged her wrist as she headed for the door. She froze, not daring to look at him. Not wanting him to see how difficult this was for her.

"Merry. We need to talk."

She laughed sharply. Fatal words, those. The last time they'd been spoken, it had been she who had insisted that they had to talk . . . she who had spilled out the wild, outrageous tale of Irish poetry and midnight dreams.

"I have to go to work," she repeated, hating the raw desperation in her voice.

He considered her for a long, humming moment. "Tonight," he said. "We'll talk tonight."

When she nodded, he reluctantly let her go.

The day alternately crawled and sped by. She wanted it over, but she didn't want to face Patrick that evening. Cory's persistent probing about Merry's uncharacteristic silence didn't help either.

And the fact that Patrick was waiting for her when she pulled into the driveway only intensified an inner tension that was already bowstring-tight.

Patrick wasn't in a mood to be put off. He was determined to set things right between them. He met her at the door. Helping her with her coat, he hung it on the hall tree. With a gentle but firm hand at the small of her back, he guided her into the living room.

She was too quiet and far too tense. He knew he was responsible on both counts. He'd bungled things badly, starting with his reaction to her story about the dreams and ending with his hurried good-bye phone call.

How could he have failed to take into account her vulnerability? She was a strong, independent woman, but she was fragile when it came to matters of the heart.

She'd confided a shocking secret to him. He'd rewarded her by doing exactly what she'd expected: listened with stunned disbelief, then left her.

Brilliant. If there was a quick fix, he was determined to find it. Starting with tonight.

"I want you to tell me again about the book."

"Patrick—"

"No more secrets between us, Merry. No more doubts. You may not like what's happened to you. Lord knows I don't like that you've gone through it alone. But the time for denial is over. Something strange has been going on in your life. I want to find out exactly what it is."

"To what end?" she asked. "It's not going to change what's happened. It's not going to make it go away."

"But it might make it easier to deal with."

"Easier for who?"

The accusation in her question cut deep, but no deeper than he deserved. He realized then just how difficult it had been for her to live with her secret. And he understood even more how much he'd hurt her.

"Merry, I'm sorry. I reacted badly when you told me about this. No excuses, but try to understand. It was a shock for me too. You've had a chance to get used to the idea. Think about it. Wasn't your first reaction denial? Isn't it still? Wouldn't you like some answers?"

She closed her eyes.

"Trust me, love."

He felt rather than sensed her desire to surrender.

"Trust me," he repeated making her look at him.

She searched his face and made her decision. "What do you want to know?"

He squeezed her hands in his. "Everything. Starting with what day of the week you bought the book, the date, the time, the bookstore. I want to know every last detail of every last dream. Every echo, every sigh, every whisper from the past that has haunted you."

TEN

The weatherman had forecast heavy winds and freezing rain moving in by midnight. Hugging her arms against a chill that whistled around the caulking, Merry stood by her kitchen window watching for Patrick's car. It was barely 8:00 P.M., and the wind had already arrived. With a vengeance.

Low gray clouds had banded together as early as dusk to cast a threatening, brooding presence on the horizon. Since then night had fallen, and the wind, if possible, had picked up even more.

Ever since the night he had insisted she outline the details of her story, Patrick had become caught up in it. Solving the puzzle had become his mission.

To that end, he enlisted all the help he could get. He and Jerry had left early that morning to comb yet another library, yet another corner of the courthouse, for more buried public records. Research, he'd said, with a determined grin, was what he did best. And so that Merry wouldn't be alone in this, he'd sicced Cory on her.

At the moment Cory was sprawled comfortably between two chairs at Merry's kitchen table. A handful of peanuts and a can of pop nearby, she thumbed through her stack of books. Elbow deep in *Psychic Voyages*, *Visions and Prophecies*, and *Spirit Summoning*, Cory was as happy as a bird in full feather.

"'To believe is to pit reason against faith,'" Cory read aloud. "See, that's why all of this is so difficult for you to accept. You, Merry Thomas, are a reasonable person. What has been happening to you is beyond the realm of reason. But *not* beyond the realm of possibility," she added emphatically. "Come on, Mer, take off your realist's hat and look at this."

Merry scowled, then diverted her gaze to Mystery. The kitten was curled up in a ball on a small braided rug Merry had placed on top of a radiator.

"Pleeeeaaaase, Merry. Just look at this one book. It has page after page, story after story, of connections and visitations and links with the past. These are documented accounts, Mer. Hundreds of them."

"And ninety-nine out of a hundred have been attacked by skeptics as delusions," Merry returned, smoothing a hand over the kitten's satin fur.

"Because people don't want to pit reason against faith," Cory argued, reemphasizing her earlier statement. "It's not a comfortable thing to do. But we're not talking here about a bunch of airheads who also dabble in nocturnal encounters with little green men who take them for rides in their spaceships. These people are credible. Among them are doctors, scientists, professors—and they've all received messages from the past."

Reluctant, but knowing Cory would wheedle until she finally wore her down, Merry sat down at the table.

Cory shoved a book under her nose. "Start here."

Resistant but resigned, Merry began to read. The accounts in the books were eerily convincing. Each documented statement eroded by inches her disbelief that unseen forces could be at work in her life.

By the time Patrick and Jerry breezed through the door on a gust of wind that seemed to have come directly from the Arctic, an uncomfortable clenching in her chest was working itself into a painful knot.

She looked up at Patrick, a part of her wanting to know what he'd found out—another part afraid.

He smiled in reassurance and bent to kiss her.

"Enough, already," Cory sputtered, making do with a quick peck and a cozy wink from Jerry. "Did you hit pay dirt?"

Patrick peeled off his jacket and reached for the coffeepot. Spinning a chair around backward, he straddled it and set his cup on the table.

"What we hit was the jackpot," he said, his gaze never leaving Merry's.

He tossed a stack of documents onto the table.

Merry stared at him, at the flash of excitement in his eyes, at his dark hair, tousled by the driving wind, at tanned cheeks mottled with red from the biting cold.

"Go ahead," he said gently, and nodded toward the papers.

Hesitantly, she picked them up, then sorted slowly through photocopies of newspaper clippings, deeds, and pages from ledgers . . . some of which bore dates back to the late 1800s. One particular document caught her attention.

She picked it up, willing her hands not to tremble. "This is a copy of the abstract to the house."

A tense silence settled over the kitchen. Jerry was the first to break it. "Come on, Cory. Let's go grab a burger somewhere."

Cory looked at Jerry as if he'd grown another muscle—right in the middle of his forehead. "Are you nuts? I want to hear this."

"I can fill you in," he said, and with gentle insistence bundled her into her coat and steered her, sputtering, toward the door.

Silent, full of dread, Merry stared blankly at the papers, then at the door as it shut soundly behind Jerry and Cory.

"It's that bad?" she asked when she and Patrick were alone.

"It's . . ." He hesitated, searching for the right words. "A bit overwhelming."

She looked from the papers to Patrick to the papers again. Shoving away from the table, she walked on unsteady legs to the stove, then to the sink, fussing unnecessarily at each stop to polish a smudge that wasn't there, to wipe at a spot on a countertop that was spotless.

"I don't know if I'm ready for this," she admitted, facing the window and away from him.

Chair legs scraped against oak flooring. She stiffened, sensing him behind her before she felt his arms enfold her.

"You're shaking."

"Something tells me I'm going to be shaking even harder before this is over."

"It'll be okay." He pressed his cheek against hers. "Come on, then. Let's have a look at what I've found out."

He settled her back down at the table and, with painstaking precision, laid it all out for her. He started with immigration records dating back to 1892, then a newspaper clipping written a year later announcing the opening of a new carriage business. Next came a copy of a building permit issued a year after that that was accompanied by a quitclaim deed to an acre lot on what was then the far outskirts of town. It was the lot on which her house was built.

With each piece of evidence the knot in Merry's chest grew tighter. A final newspaper clipping grabbed her with a merciless twist.

10 Nov., 1893. A runaway team frightened by an approaching street car turned First Avenue East into a racetrack for a short while yesterday evening. Three other teams joined in the fray

when James McFarlan, owner of McFarlan Carriage Company, was thrown from his carriage and trampled to death. McFarlan, a recent immigrant from Ireland, known to his friends simply as Jamie, was noted for his ready smile and strong work ethic. His passing will be mourned by the entire city.

She read the clipping again, aware that her hands were no longer shaking. She was past shock. She was far beyond it.

Jamie had been real. Her dream lover had been a living, breathing man. Someone's son. Someone's lover. And he'd left a lover waiting for him who had probably never learned why he hadn't come back for her.

A tear trickled unchecked down her cheek. Seeing it, Patrick covered her hands with his.

"The book?" she asked so softly, she wasn't sure if he'd heard her. "Did you find out anything about the book?"

He squeezed her hands. "It has a long history. The store where you bought it was able to trace it back to a shipment from an estate that came directly from Ireland. The owner of the store dug up some notes that accompanied the shipping invoices. One of the descendants of the estate was a merchant shipper. The book, among many other items, belonged to his daughter."

She thought of the wind chimes in her dreams.

Wind chimes Merry Clare's father had brought back from one of his voyages to the Orient.

She tried to draw her hands from Patrick's. He held on tight.

"What does it all mean?"

He studied her closely. "I think you already know."

She stared at their joined hands in helpless silence.

"Merry . . . listen to me. I know this is not an idea you embrace. The enormity of it—the logistics—it's staggering. Unbelievable. It's not easy for me either, love. But the fact remains, it exists. Whether you accept what has happened in theory or acknowledge it as fact, something—call it a force, call it fate, call it anything you want—but *something* has brought us together."

Still silent, still resistant, still staring, Merry knew what was coming, but not how to stop it.

"We've called it attraction. We've called it chemistry. We've called it everything but the one thing we both know it is."

Reincarnation . . . spiritual summoning . . . threads of a psychic tapestry. The words she'd just read in Cory's books flooded her mind. She didn't want to believe. But faced with all the proof, how could she possibly not?

"Are you saying you believe we are the means to the end of a one-hundred-year-old love affair?"

He smiled gently, and she knew he was struggling, too . . . at least with the implications attached to the dreams. What he said, however, shocked her far more than if he'd told her he'd kissed the Blarney stone and been turned into a leprechaun.

"I'm saying only one thing with certainty. I'd have found you and fallen in love with you regardless of what brought us together."

Her heart raced. Her mind bucked with denial. "Don't."

"Don't love you?"

"Don't think it."

He laughed harshly. "I don't *think* it. I feel it. I live it."

This wasn't supposed to happen. He wasn't supposed to talk about love. Neither of them were. Panic, profound and penetrating, rushed through her blood like floodwaters in a rain-swollen creek.

"You don't love me. You're just caught up in this"—she spread her hands in a helpless gesture toward the documents strewn across the table—"this fantasy. Patrick . . . please think. You're confusing fact with fiction, reality with romance."

Patrick watched her carefully. She was not handling this well. But then, he hadn't expected her to. He was a little in awe of his discoveries about Jamie McFarlan himself. And there was still more he hadn't told her, for fear of upsetting her further. Later, when she'd had time to sort this through, he would tell her the rest.

In the meantime he meant to make her understand one thing with crystal clarity: He was *not* confused. Not about his feelings for her.

"It's scary stuff, love, I know. But trust me on this

much at least. I know what I feel for you. I do love you. It's not such a bad thing," he added with a sympathetic smile when she paled. "Most people find the prospect of love incredibly wonderful. You would, too, if you'd just step back and consider the possibilities."

"I know all the possibilities." A desperate determination clouded her eyes. "They start and end with you leaving."

"Not fair, Merry. They started with your husband leaving. They ended with me. I've told you, love—I'm staying put."

She shoved out of her chair, escape on her mind. "I don't want to talk about this."

He wasn't about to let her run away from this confrontation. "We have to talk about it. You owe me that much. You owe yourself. You owe *us*."

Pacing the kitchen, she shook her head. "You don't understand."

"Try me, then."

She whirled to face him. "I've *tried* to tell you. You don't listen."

Mystery rose, stretched, and padded to the floor beside Patrick's feet. Never taking his eyes off Merry, Patrick scooped the kitten onto his lap. "The only thing you've ever tried to tell me is that you don't want to love again. Because love constitutes involvement. Well, too late, Merry. You *are* involved. I know how involved, because I'm the man who loves you. The man you trust with your body. Why do you think you can't trust me with your heart as well?"

"Because you're just like him!"

While he wasn't known for his temper, Patrick did have one. Right now, it took everything in him to check it.

"Why," he said, as the kitten sensed his anger and jumped to the floor, "do I get the feeling you're not referring to Jamie?"

She faced him bravely. "Because I'm talking about Gavin."

If she'd hit him with a baseball bat, she couldn't have staggered him more.

Seeing that, she pleaded with gentle eyes. "It's not your fault."

She wanted understanding. He gave her sarcasm instead as he felt something precious start slipping away.

"Well, that, at least, is something. Tell me, if you would be so kind, what sins your ex and I have in common."

"Patrick . . . think. Look at your life. Then look at mine. Our needs are diametrically opposite. I need home, hearth, stability. You live on the edge. You need excitement, a challenge, the opportunity to grapple with the unknown. Gavin was like that too. He was always restless for something more. Something he couldn't find with me."

He clenched his jaw. "I'm only going to say this one more time: I am not Gavin."

Her eyes softened. "He wasn't a bad man, Patrick. He was just a bad match. And so are we."

"And I'm supposed to accept your assessment of what I'd be willing to give you in a relationship based on the past you shared with your husband?"

"You're supposed to step back and look at us. At the impossibility of us. Patrick, you pick up at any whim to embark on some great adventure. You have no responsibilities, because you don't want any. I'm not faulting you for it. It's one of the things I lo—" she stopped, checking herself when she realized what she was about to say. "It's one of the things I find so special about you."

"You were going to say it was one of the things you love about me," he said quietly. "Deny it."

She took his dare and bested him.

"It was one of the things I loved about Gavin too. You have to understand—I don't want to live my life waiting for you. I don't want to wait and wonder if you'll find your way back to me. Wonder if, like Gavin, someday you'll want out for good."

He knew she hadn't meant to hurt him. In fact, he suspected she had no idea that she was capable of cutting so deep. Not only was she capable, she was lethally effective. Thirty-eight years he'd waited for a woman to commit to, and all she could do was judge him by some other man's stupidity.

"I don't want you to change," she went on in a voice that pleaded for understanding. "I don't want you to even *try* to change. You'd end up hating me for it. And I couldn't live each day knowing that when you left, it was because I had forced you to go."

"The way Gavin did," he added with a stony glare.

She looked away. "Yes."

He rose. Watching her, he snagged his jacket from the chair and slung it over his shoulder. "Well. I guess that's it, then."

He walked slowly to the door, then paused with his hand on the knob. "I'll send you a check for the rent."

"Send?"

He smiled, without humor, without a prayer. "It seems I've got another wild hair. A powerful itch to get as far away from here as possible. But then . . . I don't have to tell you about that, do I? You've already got me figured out."

Merry wasn't sure later exactly how it had happened so quickly. One minute she'd been struggling to both deny and grasp the information Patrick had gathered about the dreams, the next she'd closed herself off, shut him out, and watched him walk out of her life.

Walk? He'd practically run. She didn't blame him. She'd been ruthless. She'd been in a panic. She'd been blinded by the past, deafened by its truths, and devastated by its implications for their future.

But one recurrent message had echoed more loudly than all the others: Her relationship with Patrick was as doomed as Merry Clare's had been with Jamie. Unlike the Merry Clare of old, however, she had known in advance how it would end.

The kitchen stayed cold long after Patrick had

closed the door behind him. Long after she realized she'd shoved him out of her life and opened herself up to a loneliness more vast than anything she'd known before she'd met him.

Sometime after midnight she climbed the stairs. A long time after that she fell asleep.

The terrifying nightmare, not about Jamie and Merry Clare, but about Patrick, started shortly thereafter.

Mystery was perched at Merry's feet watching her when she reared straight up in bed.

She raked the hair out of her eyes and looked wildly around the room. Still suspended somewhere in the horror of the dream, she drew in deep drafts of air. Ignoring the sounds of the ice pelting against her windows, she threw back the covers.

One thought drove her. She had to get to him. Before it was too late, she had to get to him.

Stripping off her nightshirt, she shoved her arms into a warm sweater, tugged it over her head, and slipped into a pair of jeans. In bare feet she ran down the stairs. The clock on the mantel struck 4:00 A.M. as she hit the bottom step.

Snagging a jacket and shoes from the hall closet, she raced through the wind and rain to Patrick's door.

The cottage was dark. She didn't waste time pounding on the door, just let herself in. Once inside, she flipped on a light and headed for his bedroom.

As she'd feared, his bed was not only empty, it

hadn't been slept in. She flung open the closet door. His duffel was gone.

Jerry. Jerry would know where to find him . . . before it was too late.

Flipping on lights as she went, Merry rushed from room to room until she found a phone book. It came as no surprise to her that Jerry's number wasn't listed.

Pressing a hand to her pounding heart, she paused before his office door. After a moment's hesitation she let herself inside.

Feeling like a felon but no longer caring, she riffled through Patrick's desk until she found what she was looking for. His address book was distinctive and organized. Flipping quickly through the pages, she found Jerry's number and punched out the digits.

"Come on, come on, answer the phone," she whispered impatiently as she counted off the rings.

" 'lo?" A woman's voice, groggy with sleep, finally answered. In her urgency it took a moment for Merry to identify the voice.

"Cory? Cory, it's Merry. Don't ask questions. Just let me talk to Jerry."

"Merry . . . what's wrong? Good grief, it's . . . oh, for Pete's sake . . . it's four-fifteen. What—"

"Put Jerry on the phone!"

Muffled whispers filtered through the receiver before Jerry came on the line. "Merry . . . what's the problem?"

"Patrick's gone. Jerry, I've got to find him. Do you know where he went?"

"To lick his wounds."

His tone and words cut deep. "I don't have time for this, Jerry. Please, just tell me where he is."

She squeezed her eyes shut as Jerry filled her in, fleshing out the images of the dream that had awakened her. She didn't waste time with good-byes but abruptly disconnected. Her fingers raced over the address book until she found the number for the airport.

A quick call confirmed a 4:45 A.M. flight with connections to South America. A glance at the wall clock told her she had a slim chance of making it to the airport before departure time.

She whirled for the door, banged her hip on the desk, and in the process of steadying herself knocked a book to the floor.

Swearing softly, she kicked it out of her way and raced out of the room. She stopped short just outside the threshold as a startling awareness enveloped her.

Turning on her heel, she walked haltingly back into the room. With shaking hands, she picked up the book, staring in stunned disbelief at the author's name on the jacket cover. Even before she turned the book over, she knew whose face she'd see on the back of the book jacket.

Numbed by her discovery, she scanned the desk and spotted the other books . . . books she hadn't noticed that fateful night she'd wandered into his office in search of something to help her unwind. The night Patrick had come into her life.

She recognized some of the titles. In some distant corner of her mind she even recalled seeing some of them on best-seller lists in newspapers over the years.

Bracing herself, she tucked the book under her arm and raced out of the house into the freezing rain.

Dog-tired and too rapidly edging toward hangover status, Patrick felt as cranky as a pit bull leashed to a log chain.

The damn flight was late. Why was he not surprised? He slumped lower in the chrome-and-vinyl seat in the terminal waiting room, cursing the weather, his failing Irish luck, and life in general.

He didn't want to go anywhere. Yet here he was, ready to board a plane that would take him to God only knew what in the jungles of South America. He was getting too damn old for this. Just his luck he'd fallen in love with a stubborn, wounded woman who didn't want to hear that he was tired of his restless ways.

He'd just managed to doze off when something hit him with a thud in his gut.

He shot out of the chair, eyes wild, clutching his stomach and the—what the hell? The missile that had hit him was a book—*his* book. He'd fielded his share of industrious fans requesting autographs, but this one had gone a bit too far.

In bleary-eyed anger he frowned, first at the book,

hen at the woman who had thrown it. When he saw
hat the fiery and beautiful eyes glaring back at him
were Merry's, his anger cooled and his heartbeat quick-
ned.

Her hair hung in wet ringlets about her face. The
cy wind had painted her cheeks a vivid berry red. And
her eyes—her expressive heather-gray eyes—were
hooting daggers . . . all aimed directly at him.

He felt immeasurably better, but he wasn't about to
et her know it. Her presence here told him what he
heeded to know. He wasn't sure, though, if *she* was
completely aware of her reason for coming after him.
Much as he wanted to wrap her in his arms and do the
explaining for her, the words had to come from her.

A violent shudder racked her as a chill from her wet
clothes penetrated her body. Steeling himself against
he urge to shelter her against him, he kept his distance
and dug deep for a scowl. "Out and about a bit early,
aren't you, love?"

"You bastard."

He shrugged. "I've never pretended to be otherwise. Did you have something on your mind, then?" he
asked when she stood in shivering silence.

"You were really going to leave, weren't you?"

He wanted to believe there was some sorrow laced
with her rage. "Well, I try like hell to live up to your
expectations."

That put her in a fine snit. Her cheeks maintained
their pretty pink as she glared at him, then at the book.
"Why didn't you tell me?"

He followed her gaze. "That I was an author? I believe I did."

"That you were a *successful* author," she clarified bitingly.

"What? And spoil the starving-artist illusion you seemed to treasure?" He shrugged. "Didn't seem necessary."

She shoved a wet fall of hair away from her face. "Why didn't you tell me who you were?"

A passing traveler gave her dripping clothes and flashing eyes the once-over. She ignored him.

"You know who I am," Patrick said, and glanced down at the book. "My pen name didn't seem important."

"It's important."

He saw it then, the frustration battling with the hurt as she squared off against him.

"It was especially important last night. Why didn't you tell me then?"

He watched her carefully. "If I recall, you decided it was time for me to leave before I got a chance to tell you."

She looked away, guilt—and, if he could believe his interpretations, regret—darkening her eyes. She stared at the book instead of him.

He spoke to her lowered head. "Choosing James McFarlan as my pseudonym all those years ago wasn't entirely coincidental. James is my middle name, Mc-Farlan my mother's maiden name. But you can blame my agent—he thought the combination looked better on a book jacket than Patrick Ryan."

Shivering, she hugged her arms around her waist, damning him and yet somehow pleading with her eyes.

"There's something else you didn't let me finish last night, Merry." He dug into the breast pocket of his jacket. Taking her cold hand in his, he pressed a small velvet pouch into her palm.

She stared at it.

"Go ahead. Look inside. Something tells me you already know, though, what you'll find."

With trembling fingers she tugged open the drawstring on the faded purple velvet and emptied the contents of the pouch into her palm.

She paled. A golden locket suspended from a delicate tangle of finely woven gold chain lay in the palm of her shaking hand. "Merry's locket," she whispered breathlessly.

"Your locket," he said quietly, meaningfully.

"How . . . where . . . ?"

"The how and the where don't matter. Not anymore. What matters is why. Why are you here, Merry? Why did you come looking for me?"

Closing her fingers around the locket, she seemed to snap out of her shock and remember her purpose. Her eyes flared again. Had he not been so determined to force her hand, he would have dragged her into his arms and said the hell with it. He had enough love to do the convincing for both of them.

But he steeled himself, knowing it had to come from her.

"Why, Merry?" he repeated with a scowl to match hers.

"Because I wanted to warn you, you arrogant Irish bastard."

He cocked an eyebrow that helped camouflage a grin. "Warn me?"

She was quiet for a moment, and he sensed her inner struggle. "To warn you not to go . . . wherever it is you're going. Just don't," she said finally.

"Why? Because you'd miss me?"

"Because if you go . . . you might be hurt."

He frowned, then understood. "Another dream, Merry?"

She didn't answer. Her silence was enough confirmation for him.

"So the dreams won't let you alone," he concluded. "Well, don't worry yourself on my account. You've issued your warning. You've done your duty. If that's all you had on your mind, you'd best go home. Get out of those wet clothes before you catch a cold."

A flight was called over the loudspeaker.

"That'll be me," he said, picking up his duffel.

He watched her face. The emotions were there, but the words weren't coming. One word—the right word—and he'd walk away *with* her, not away *from* her. But the word had to come from her. When it didn't, he turned and strode purposefully toward the line of passengers preparing to board the plane.

A thousand steps seemed to click off, a million seconds to tick by, and still she didn't call his name.

He'd blown it. He was walking away from the best thing in his life, and the only real barrier keeping them apart had turned out to be his pride.

A man was nothing without his pride.

"Patrick . . ."

He stopped, physically suppressing a shudder of relief.

Without turning around, he waited.

"Don't go. . . ." she said finally in a voice made reedy by hesitation.

He turned slowly, facing her across twenty yards of glaring lights and polished tile and her damnable uncertainty.

"Why?" he asked point-blank.

She swallowed, shooting a misty-eyed gaze toward the ceiling, then back at him. "Because it could be dangerous."

He shook his head sadly. "Not good enough."

She looked away again, then with a deep sigh met his eyes. "Because I don't want you to go," she said in a small voice.

"Why?" he repeated, softer this time as his anxious heart pumped blood through his ears and threatened to drown out her reply.

"Because . . ." She bit her lower lip, then pulled herself together. "Because I love you, damn you."

The last call for his flight blared from the loudspeaker.

A slow smile fought to escape the bounds of his carefully nurtured scowl. "I . . . don't believe I caught that. Do you suppose you could repeat it, love?"

He knew that in that moment she read his look for what it was—an unconcealed combination of relief, joy, and victorious teasing.

She started walking slowly toward him. "Because I love you," she stated loud and clear, then broke into a smile that made his heart sing. "Because I love you," she repeated as she launched herself into his arms.

He dropped his duffel, catching her tightly against him.

"Because you aren't Gavin, because you are Patrick, and I love your roguish smile and devil-black eyes and your damnable Irish charm. Because," she continued between kisses, "you love me and you can't live without me and because I know that unless I give you good reason, you'll never leave me."

"Finally," he said, kissing her again, not caring about the shaking heads and knowing smiles of the boarding passengers. "Finally, you've got it right."

"What Cory said was true," she whispered, framing his face with her hands. "I was trying to pit reason against faith, when all along I didn't need a reason. I just needed you and the faith to risk my heart on the chance that you needed me too."

"Well, then"—he smiled into her eyes—"I guess that goes to show you: You should have paid more attention to your dreams. If you had, you'd have known there was never any risk involved. Where you're concerned, Merry, I've always been a sure thing."

"I love you," she whispered, searching his face, baring her soul.

"And don't you ever forget it." He wrapped her against him and held on tight. "Come on then. Let's go home."

EPILOGUE

The scent of the sea and heather hung heavily in the morning mist. The air that crept in through the slightly open window and into the honeymoon suite of the seaside inn brought with it a chill from last night's rain.

Merry snuggled deeper into the covers and the warmth of Patrick's body. After a long, lazy moment she opened her eyes and focused on the book of poetry lying open on the bedside table.

Beside, her, Patrick shifted. She turned her head on the pillow to see that he was awake and watching her.

"Top 'o the mornin', Mrs. Ryan," he whispered, brushing the hair back from her eyes with a gentle hand. "And aren't you a pur and lovely sight for the likes of these eyes of mine?"

She envisioned her tangled hair and bleary eyes, which undoubtedly showed the wear of a night short on sleep and long on loving. "That's one of the things I love about you, Patrick," she murmured with a sleepy smile. "You can lie with a straight face."

He rolled to his side and, tugging her with him, wrapped her tightly against him. "There's where you're wrong, lass. I'll never lie. Not to you. And Lord, you are lovely."

He kissed her, then lay back on the pillow, idly running a finger along the fine gold chain that held her locket.

"You never did tell me where you found this," she said, covering the hand that held the locket with hers.

"Think a moment. You'll figure it out."

She thought, then smiled. "It was in the chest."

"In a little compartment in the lid. After I found out Jamie had built the house, I went back to the attic to search for more clues. I found the locket instead."

She sighed and shook her head. "It's incredible, really, when you think about it—how everything pieced itself together. Even Mystery played a part in solving the puzzle."

"I wonder how the little beggar is getting on."

"I'm sure Jerry and Cory are taking great care of him."

"Speaking of taking care"—he kissed her again, sweet and slow—"I'd like to take care to keep you in this bed and under this quilt for the better part of a year. Maybe by then I'll have made a dent in my need to make love to you."

It was voracious, this need he seemed to have for her. Voracious and wonderful and real. How she'd ever doubted his love, she didn't know. He'd proved it again and again.

"It sounds wonderful," she said, feeling the stirrings of a need of her own, "but something tells me that your family might be a wee bit upset if we don't show up on their doorstep by this time next week."

He grinned. "There is that. They're going to love you, you know. And as long as they don't find out we've been in Ireland for the better part of a week before we put in an appearance, they'll be happy to see me too. Pure selfishness on my part, I know, but I wanted to show you Ireland myself, before the Ryan clan converges to welcome you to the fold."

"I love Ireland."

"Ireland loves you," he said, "and this Irishman loves you most of all."

Her heart reacted to the warmth in his eyes. "It's strange, you know? From the moment I set foot on Irish soil, I've felt a sense of home. Of homecoming."

In silence, in communion, they thought of the dreams that brought them together and that had finally brought them here.

"I dreamed of them last night . . . of Jamie and Merry Clare. I hadn't heard from them since the first time we made love."

He was strangely quiet. "And what did you dream, love?"

"It was different this time . . . more of a feeling than an image."

"A feeling of contentment?"

"Yes."

"And of peace," he added, watching her eyes as he echoed her thoughts with uncanny accuracy.

She realized then why he understood.

"You had the dream, too, didn't you."

He toyed with a strand of her hair. "I guess they wanted me to know, too, how happy they are . . . that because of us they're finally together."

Her eyes misted with sudden tears . . . tears for lovers lost, for lovers finally found.

"I don't think we'll hear from them again, love. I sensed that they were saying good-bye."

"I can't believe I'm actually saying this, but I'll miss them. And I'm sorry I never got to thank them for bringing us together."

"I thanked them for you." He rolled her beneath him, his dark eyes brimming with love and desire. "And now, I want to show you just how thankful I am that we didn't have to wait a hundred years to find each other."

Wrapping her arms around him, she opened herself completely, embracing his love, welcoming his body as he filled her with stunning measures of both. Losing themselves in each other and in the treasure of this misty morning, they made tender love and precious memories.

A skiff of wind snuck in through the window, fluttering the pages of the leather-bound book until it opened to the poem that had touched their lives and their hearts like a kind and benevolent friend.

Dream Tide

How sweetly lies old Ireland
emerald green beyond the foam,
awakening sweet memories,
calling the heart back home.

THE EDITOR'S CORNER

Let the fires of love's passion keep you warm as summer's days shorten into the frosty nights of autumn. Those falling leaves and chilly mornings are a sure signal that winter's on the way! So make a date to snuggle up under a comforter and read the six romances LOVESWEPT has in store for you. They're sure to heat up your reading hours with their witty and sensuous tales.

Fayrene Preston's scrumptious and clever story, **THE COLORS OF JOY,** LOVESWEPT #642 is a surefire heartwarmer. Seemingly unaware of his surroundings, Caleb McClintock steps off the curb—and is yanked out of the path of an oncoming car by a blue-eyed angel! Even though Joy Williams had been pretending to be her twin sister as part of a daredevil charade, he'd recognized her, known her when almost no one could tell them apart. His wickedly sensual experiments will surely show a lady who's adored variety that one man is all she'll ever need! You won't soon forget this charming story by Fayrene.

Take a trip to the tropics with Linda Wisdom's **SUDDEN IMPULSE**, LOVESWEPT #643. Ben Wyatt had imagined the creator of vivid fabric designs as a passionate wanton who wove her fiery fantasies into the cloth of dreams, but when he flew to Treasure Cove to meet her, he was shocked to encounter Kelly Andrews, a cool businesswoman who'd chosen paradise as an escape! Beguiled by the tawny-eyed designer who'd sworn off driven men wedded to their work, Ben sensed that beneath her silken surface was a fire he must taste. Captivated by her beauty, enthralled by her sensuality, Ben challenged her to seize her chance at love. Linda's steamy tale will melt away the frost of a chilly autumn day.

Theresa Gladden will get you in the Halloween mood with her spooky but oh, so sexy duo, **ANGIE AND THE GHOSTBUSTER**, LOVESWEPT #644. Drawn to an old house by an intriguing letter and a shockingly vivid dream, Dr. Gabriel Richards came in search of a tormented ghost—but instead found a sassy blonde with dreamer's eyes who awakened an old torment of his own. Angie Parker was two-parts angel to one-part vixen, a sexy, skeptical, single mom who suspected a con—but couldn't deny the chemistry between them, or disguise her burning need. Theresa puts her "supernatural" talents to their best use in this delightful tale.

The ever-creative and talented Judy Gill returns with a magnificent, touching tale that I'm sure you'll agree is a **SHEER DELIGHT**, LOVESWEPT #645. Matt Fiedler had been caught looking—and touching—the silky lingerie on display in the sweet-scented boutique, but when he discovered he'd stumbled into Dee Farris's shop, he wanted his hands all over the lady instead! Dee had never forgotten the reckless bad boy who'd awakened her to exquisite passion in college, then shattered her dreams by promising to return for her, but never keeping his word. Dee feared the doubts that had once driven him away couldn't be silenced by desire, that Matt's pride might be stronger than his need to possess her. This one will grab hold of your heartstrings and never let go!

Victoria Leigh's in brilliant form with **TAKE A CHANCE ON LOVE**, LOVESWEPT #646. Biff Fuller could almost taste her skin and smell her exotic fragrance from across the casino floor, but he sensed that the bare-shouldered woman gambling with such abandon might be the most dangerous risk he'd ever taken! Amanda Lawrence never expected to see him again, the man who'd branded her his with only a touch. But when Biff appeared without warning and vowed to fight her dragons, she had to surrender. The emotional tension in Vicki's very special story will leave you breathless!

I'm sure that you must have loved Bonnie Pega's first book with us last summer. I'm happy to say that she's outdoing herself with her second great love story, **WILD THING**, LOVESWEPT #647. Patrick Brady knew he'd had a concussion, but was the woman he saw only a hazy fantasy, or delectable flesh and blood? Robin McKenna wasn't thrilled about caring for the man, even less when she learned her handsome patient was a reporter—but she was helpless to resist his long, lean body and his wicked grin. Seduced by searing embraces and tantalized by unbearable longing, Robin wondered if she dared confess the truth. Trusting Patrick meant surrendering her sorrow, but could he show her she was brave enough to claim his love forever? Bonnie's on her way to becoming one of your LOVESWEPT favorites with **WILD THING**.

Here's to the fresh, cool days—and hot nights—of fall.

With best wishes,

Nita Taublib

Nita Taublib
Associate Publisher

P.S. Don't miss the exciting big women's fiction reads Bantam will have on sale in September: Teresa Medeiros's **A WHISPER OF ROSES,** Rosanne Bittner's **TENDER BETRAYAL,** Lucia Grahame's **THE PAINTED LADY,** and Sara Orwig's **OREGON BROWN.** We'll be giving you a sneak peek at these terrific books in next month's LOVESWEPTS. And immediately following this page look for a preview of the spectacular women's fiction books from Bantam *available now!*

Iris Johansen

nationally bestselling author of
THE TIGER PRINCE

presents

THE MAGNIFICENT ROGUE

Iris Johansen's spellbinding, sensuous romantic novels have captivated readers and won awards for a decade now, and this is her most spectacular story yet. From the glittering court of Queen Elizabeth to a barren Scottish island, here is a heartstopping tale of courageous love . . . and unspeakable evil.

The daring chieftain of a Scottish clan, Robert McDarren knows no fear, and only the threat to a kinsman's life makes him bow to Queen Elizabeth's order that he wed Kathryn Ann Kentrye. He's aware of the dangerous secret in Kate's past, a secret that could destroy a great empire, but he doesn't expect the stirring of desire when he first lays eyes on the fragile beauty. Grateful to escape the tyranny of her guardian, Kate accepts the mesmerizing stranger as her husband. But even as they discover a passion greater than either has known, enemies are weaving their poisonous web around them, and soon Robert and Kate must risk their very lives to defy the ultimate treachery.

"I won't hush. You cannot push me away again. I tell you that—"

Robert covered her lips with his hand. "I know what you're saying. You're saying I don't have to shelter you under my wing but I must coo like a peaceful dove whenever I'm around you."

"I could not imagine you cooing, but I do not think peace and friendship between us is too much to ask." She blinked rapidly as she moved her head to avoid his hand. "You promised that—"

"I know what I promised and you have no right to ask more from me. You can't expect to beckon me close and then have me keep my distance," he said harshly. "You can't have it both ways, as you would know if you weren't—" He broke off. "And for God's sake don't *weep*."

"I'm not weeping."

"By God, you are."

"I have something in my eye. You're not being sensible."

"I'm being more sensible than you know," he said with exasperation. "Christ, why the devil is this so important to you?"

She wasn't sure except that it had something to do with that wondrous feeling of *rightness* she had experienced last night. She had never known it before and she would not give it up. She tried to put it into words. "I feel as if I've been closed up inside for a long time. Now I want . . . something else. It will do you no harm to be my friend."

"That's not all you want," he said slowly as he studied her desperate expression. "I don't think you know what you want. But I do and I can't give it to you."

"You could try." She drew a deep breath. "Do you think it's easy for me to ask this of you? It fills me with anger and helplessness and I *hate* that feeling."

She wasn't reaching him. She had to say something that would convince him. Suddenly the words came tumbling out, words she had never meant to say, expressing emotions she had never realized she felt. "I thought all I'd need would be a house but now I know there's something more. I have to have people too. I guess I always knew it but the house was easier, safer. Can't you see? I want what you and Gavin and Angus have, and I don't know if I can find it alone. Sebastian told me I couldn't have it but I will. I *will*." Her hands nervously clenched and unclenched at her sides. "I'm all tight inside. I feel scorched . . . like a desert. Sebastian made me this way and I don't know how to stop. I'm not . . . at ease with anyone."

He smiled ironically. "I've noticed a certain lack of trust in me but you seem to have no problem with Gavin."

"I truly like Gavin but he can't change what I am," she answered, then went on eagerly. "It was different with you last night, though. I really *talked* to you. You made me feel . . ." She stopped. She had sacrificed enough of her pride. If this was not enough, she could give no more.

The only emotion she could identify in the multitude of expressions that flickered across his face was frustration. And there was something else, something darker, more intense. He threw up his hands. "All right, I'll try."

Joy flooded through her. "Truly?"

"My God, you're obstinate."

"It's the only way to keep what one has. If I hadn't fought, you'd have walked away."

"I see." She had the uneasy feeling he saw more than her words had portended. But she must accept this subtle intrusion of apprehension if she was to be fully accepted by him.

"Do I have to make a solemn vow?" he asked with a quizzical lift of his brows.

"Yes, please. Truly?" she persisted.

"Truly." Some of the exasperation left his face. "Satisfied?"

"Yes, that's all I want."

"Is it?" He smiled crookedly. "That's not all I want."

The air between them was suddenly thick and hard to breathe, and Kate could feel the heat burn in her cheeks. She swallowed. "I'm sure you'll get over that once you become accustomed to thinking of me differently."

He didn't answer.

"You'll see." She smiled determinedly and quickly changed the subject. "Where is Gavin?"

"In the kitchen fetching food for the trail."

"I'll go find him and tell him you wish to leave at—"

"In a moment." He moved to stand in front of her and lifted the hood of her cape, then framed her face with a gesture that held a possessive intimacy. He looked down at her, holding her gaze. "This is not a wise thing. I don't know how long I can stand this box you've put me in. All I can promise is that I'll give you warning when I decide to break down the walls."

VIRTUE
by
Jane Feather

"GOLD 5 stars." —*Heartland Critiques*

"An instantaneous attention-grabber. A well-crafted romance with a strong, compelling story and utterly delightful characters." —*Romantic Times*

VIRTUE is the newest regency romance from Jane Feather, four-time winner of Romantic Times's *Reviewer's Choice award, and author of the national bestseller* The Eagle and the Dove.

With a highly sensual style reminiscent of Amanda Quick and Karen Robards, Jane Feather works her bestselling romantic magic with this tale of a strong-willed beauty forced to make her living at the gaming tables, and the arrogant nobleman determined to get the better of her— with passion. The stakes are nothing less than her VIRTUE . . .

What the devil was she doing? Marcus Devlin, the most honorable Marquis of Carrington, absently exchanged his empty champagne glass for a full one as a flunkey passed him. He pushed his shoulders off the wall, straightening to his full height, the better to see across the crowded room to the macao table. She was up to something. Every prickling hair on the nape of his neck told him so.

She was standing behind Charlie's chair, her fan moving in slow sweeps across the lower part of her face. She leaned forward to whisper something in Charlie's ear, and the rich swell of her breasts, the deep shadow of the cleft between them, was uninhibitedly revealed in the décolletage of her evening gown. Charlie looked up at her and smiled, the soft, infatuated smile of puppy love. It wasn't surprising this young cousin had fallen head over heels for Miss Judith Davenport, the marquis reflected. There was hardly a man in Brussels who wasn't stirred by her: a creature of opposites, vibrant, ebullient, sharply intelligent—a woman who in some indefinable fashion challenged a man, put him on his mettle one minute, and yet the next was as appealing as a kitten; a man wanted to pick her up and cuddle her, protect her from the storm . . .

Romantic nonsense! The marquis castigated himself severely for sounding like his cousin and half the young soldiers proudly sporting their regimentals in the salons of Brussels as the world waited for Napoleon to make his move. He'd been watching Judith Davenport weaving her spells for several weeks now, convinced she was an artful minx with a very clear agenda of her own. But for the life of him, he couldn't discover what it was.

His eyes rested on the young man sitting opposite Charlie. Sebastian Davenport held the bank. As beautiful as his sister in his own way, he sprawled in his chair, both clothing and posture radiating a studied carelessness. He was laughing across the table, lightly ruffling the cards in his hands. The mood at the table was lighthearted. It was a mood that always accompanied the Davenports. Presumably one reason why they were so popular . . . and then the marquis saw it.

It was the movement of her fan. There was a pattern to the slow sweeping motion. Sometimes the movement speeded, sometimes it paused, once or twice she snapped the fan closed, then almost immediately began a more vigorous wafting of the delicately painted half moon. There was renewed laughter at the table, and with a lazy sweep of his rake, Sebastian Davenport scooped toward him the pile of vowels and rouleaux in the center of the table.

The marquis walked across the room. As he reached the table, Charlie looked up with a rueful grin. "It's not my night, Marcus."

"It rarely is," Carrington said, taking snuff. "Be careful you don't find yourself in debt." Charlie heard the warning in the advice, for all that his cousin's voice was affably casual. A slight flush tinged the young man's cheekbones and he dropped his eyes to his cards again. Marcus was his guardian and tended to be unsympathetic when Charlie's gaming debts outran his quarterly allowance.

"Do you care to play, Lord Carrington?" Judith Davenport's soft voice spoke at the marquis's shoulder and he turned to look at her. She was smiling, her golden brown eyes luminous, framed in the thickest, curliest eyelashes he had ever seen. However, ten years spent avoiding the frequently blatant blandishments of maidens on the lookout for a rich husband had inured him to the cajolery of a pair of fine eyes.

"No. I suspect it wouldn't be my night either, Miss Davenport. *May* I escort you to the supper room? It must grow tedious, watching my cousin losing hand over fist." He offered a small bow and took her elbow without waiting for a response.

Judith stiffened, feeling the pressure of his hand cupping her bare arm. There was a hardness in his eyes that matched the firmness of his grip, and her scalp contracted as unease shivered across her skin. "On the contrary, my lord, I find the play most entertaining." She gave her arm a covert, experimental tug. His fingers gripped warmly and yet more firmly.

"But I insist, Miss Davenport. You will enjoy a glass of negus."

He had very black eyes and they carried a most unpleasant glitter, as insistent as his tone and words, both of which were drawing a degree of puzzled attention. Judith could see no discreet, graceful escape route. She laughed lightly. "You have convinced me, sir. But I prefer burnt champagne to negus."

"Easily arranged." He drew her arm through his and laid his free hand over hers, resting on his black silk sleeve. Judith felt manacled.

They walked through the card room in a silence that was as uncomfortable as it was pregnant. Had he guessed what was going on? Had he seen anything? How could she have given herself away? Or was it something Sebastian had done, said, looked . . . ? The questions and speculations raced through Judith's brain. She was barely acquainted with Marcus Devlin. He was too sophisticated, too hardheaded to be of use to herself and Sebastian, but she had the distinct sense that he would be an opponent to be reckoned with.

The supper room lay beyond the ballroom, but instead of guiding his companion around the waltzing couples and the ranks of seated chaperones against the wall, Marcus turned aside toward the long French windows opening onto a flagged terrace. A breeze stirred the heavy velvet curtains over an open door.

"I was under the impression we were going to have supper." Judith stopped abruptly.

"No, we're going to take a stroll in the night air," her escort informed her with a bland smile. "Do put one foot in front of the other, my dear ma'am, otherwise our progress might become a little uneven." An unmistakable jerk on her arm drew her forward with a stumble, and Judith rapidly adjusted her gait to match the leisured, purposeful stroll of her companion.

"I don't care for the night air," she hissed through her teeth, keeping a smile on her face. "It's very bad for the constitution and frequently results in the ague or rheumatism."

"Only for those in their dotage," he said, lifting thick black eyebrows. "I would have said you were not a day above twenty-two. Unless you're very skilled with powder and paint?"

He'd pinpointed her age exactly and the sense of being dismayingly out of her depth was intensified. "I'm not quite such an accomplished actress, my lord," she said coldly.

"Are you not?" He held the curtain aside for her and she found herself out on the terrace, lit by flambeaux set in sconces at intervals along the low parapet fronting the sweep of green lawn. "I would have sworn you were as accomplished as any on Drury Lane." The statement was accompanied by a penetrating stare.

Judith rallied her forces and responded to the comment as if it were a humorous compliment. "You're too kind, sir. I confess I've long envied the talent of Mrs. Siddons."

"Oh, you underestimate yourself," he said softly. They had reached the parapet and he stopped under the light of a torch. "You are playing some very pretty theatricals, Miss Davenport, you and your brother."

Judith drew herself up to her full height. It wasn't a

particularly impressive move when compared with her escort's breadth and stature, but it gave her an illusion of hauteur. "I don't know what you're talking about, my lord. It seems you've obliged me to accompany you in order to insult me with vague innuendoes."

"No, there's nothing vague about my accusations," he said. "However insulting they may be. I am assuming my cousin's card play will improve in your absence."

"What are you implying?" The color ebbed in her cheeks, then flooded back in a hot and revealing wave. Hastily she employed her fan in an effort to conceal her agitation.

The marquis caught her wrist and deftly twisted the fan from her hand. "You're most expert with a fan, madam."

"I beg your pardon?" She tried again for a lofty incomprehension, but with increasing lack of conviction.

"Don't continue this charade, Miss Davenport. It benefits neither of us. You and your brother may fleece as many fools as you can find as far as I'm concerned, but you'll leave my cousin alone."

Beneath a Sapphire Sea
by
Jessica Bryan
Rave reviews for Ms. Bryan's novels:

DAWN ON A JADE SEA

"Sensational! Fantastic! There are not enough super-latives to describe this romantic fantasy. A keeper!"
—*Rendezvous*

"An extraordinary tale of adventure, mystery and magic." —*Rave Reviews*

ACROSS A WINE-DARK SEA

"Thoroughly absorbing . . . A good read and a prom-ising new author!" —*Nationally bestselling author Anne McCaffrey*

Beneath the shimmering, sunlit surface of the ocean there lives a race of rare and wondrous men and women. They have walked upon the land, but their true heritage is as beings of the sea. Now their people face a grave peril. And one woman holds the key to their survival. . . .

A scholar of sea lore, Meredith came to a Greek island to follow her academic pursuits. But when she encountered Galen, a proud, determined warrior of the sea, she was eternally linked with a world far more elusive and mysteri-ously seductive than her own. For she alone possessed a scroll that held the secrets of his people.

In the following scene, Meredith has just caught Galen searching for the mysterious scroll. His reaction catches them both by surprise . . .

He drew her closer, and Meredith did not resist. To look away from his face had become impossible. She felt some-thing in him reach out for her, and something in her answered. It rose up in her like a tide, compelling beyond reason or thought. She lifted her arms and slowly put them around his broad shoulders. He tensed, as if she had startled him, then his whole body seemed to envelop hers as he pulled her against him and lowered his lips to hers.

His arms were like bands of steel, the thud of his heart deep and powerful as a drum, beating in a wild rhythm that echoed the same frantic cadence of Meredith's. His lips seared over hers. His breath was hot in her mouth, and the hard muscles of his bare upper thighs thrust against her lower belly, the bulge between them only lightly concealed by the thin material of his shorts.

Then, as quickly as their lips had come together, they parted.

Galen stared down into Meredith's face, his arms still locked around her slim, strong back. He was deeply shaken, far more than he cared to admit, even to himself. He had been totally focused on probing the landwoman's mind once and for all. Where had the driving urge to kiss her come from, descending on him with a need so strong it had overridden everything else?

He dropped his arms. "That was a mistake," he said, frowning. "I—"

"You're right." Whatever had taken hold of Meredith vanished like the "pop" of a soap bubble, leaving her feeling as though she had fallen headfirst into a cold sea. "It *was* a mistake," she said quickly. "Mine. Now if you'll just get out of here, we can both forget this unfortunate incident ever happened."

She stepped back from him, and Galen saw the anger in her eyes and, held deep below that anger, the hurt. It stung him. None of this was her fault. Whatever forces she exerted upon him, he was convinced she was completely unaware of them. He was equally certain she had no idea of the scroll's significance. To her it was simply an impressive artifact, a rare find that would no doubt gain her great recognition in this folklore profession of hers.

He could not allow that, of course. But the methods he had expected to succeed with her had not worked. He could try again—the very thought of pulling her back into her arms was a seductive one. It played on his senses with heady anticipation, shocking him at how easily this woman could distract him. He would have to find another less physical means of discovering where the scroll was.

"I did not mean it that way," he began in a gentle tone.

Meredith shook her head, refusing to be mollified. She was as taken aback as he by what had happened, and deeply chagrined as well. The fact that she had enjoyed the kiss—No, that was too calm a way of describing it. Galen's mouth had sent rivers of sensations coursing through her, sensations she had not known existed, and that just made the chagrin worse.

"I don't care what you meant," she said in a voice as stiff as her posture. "I've asked you to leave. I don't want to tell you again."

"Meredith, wait." He stepped forward, stopping just short of touching her. "I'm sorry about . . . Please believe my last wish is to offend you. But it does not change the fact that I still want to work with you. And whether you admit it or not, you need me."

"Need you?" Her tone grew frosty. "I don't see how."

"Then you don't see very much," he snapped. He paused to draw in a deep breath, then continued in a placating tone. "Who else can interpret the language on this sheet of paper for you?"

Meredith eyed him. If he was telling the truth, if he really could make sense out on those characters, then, despite the problems he presented, he was an answer to her prayers, to this obsession that would not let her go. She bent and picked up the fallen piece of paper.

"Prove it." She held it out to him. "What does this say?"

He ignored the paper, staring steadily at her. "We will work together, then?"

She frowned as she returned his stare, trying to probe whatever lay behind his handsome face. "Why is it so important to you that we do? I can see why you might think I need you, but what do you get out of this? What do you want, Galen?"

He took the paper from her. *"The season of destruction will soon be upon us and our city,"* he read deliberately, *"but I may have found a way to save some of us, we who were once among the most powerful in the sea. Near the long and narrow island that is but a stone's throw from Crete, the island split by Mother Ocean into two halves . . ."*

He stopped. "It ends there." His voice was low and fierce, as fierce as his gaze, which seemed to reach out to grip her. "Are you satisfied now? Or do you require still more proof?"

TEMPTING EDEN
by
Maureen Reynolds

author of SMOKE EYES

"Ms. Reynolds blends steamy sensuality with
marvelous lovers. . . . delightful."
—*Romantic Times on SMOKE EYES*

*Eden Victoria Lindsay knew it was foolish to break into the
home of one of New York's most famous—and reclusive—
private investigators. Now she had fifteen minutes to convince him that he shouldn't have her thrown in prison.*

*Shane O'Connor hardly knew what to make of the flaxen-
haired aristocrat who'd scaled the wall of his Long Island
mansion—except that she was in more danger than she
suspected. In his line of work, trusting the wrong woman
could get a man killed, but Shane is about to himself get
taken in by this alluring and unconventional beauty. . . .*

"She scaled the wall, sir," said Simon, Shane's stern
butler.

Eden rolled her eyes. "Yes—yes, I did! And I'd do it
again—a hundred times. How else could I reach the
impossible *inaccessible* Mr. O'Connor?"

He watched her with a quiet intensity but it was Simon
who answered, "If one wishes to speak with Mr. O'Connor, a meeting is usually arranged through the *proper*
channels."

Honestly, Eden thought, the English aristocracy did
not look down their noses half so well as these two!

O'Connor stepped gracefully out of the light and his

gaze, falling upon her, was like the steel of gunmetal. He leaned casually against the wall—his weight on one hip, his hands in his trousers pockets—and he studied her with half-veiled eyes.

"Have you informed the . . . ah . . . *lady*, Simon, what type of reception our unexpected guests might anticipate? Especially," he added in a deceptively soft tone, "those who scale the estate walls, and . . . er . . . shed their clothing?"

Eden stiffened, her face hot with color; he'd made it sound as if it were *commonplace* for women to scale his wall and undress.

Simon replied, "Ah, no, sir. In the melee, that particular formality slipped my mind."

"Do you suppose we should strip her first, or just torture her?"

"*What?*"

"Or would you rather we just arrest you, madame?"

"Sir, with your attitude it is a wonder you have a practice at all!"

"It is a wonder," he drawled coldly, "that you are still alive, madame. You're a damn fool to risk your neck as you did. Men have been shot merely for attempting it, and I'm amazed you weren't killed yourself."

Eden brightened. "Then I am to be commended, am I not? Congratulate me, sir, for accomplishing such a feat!"

Shane stared at her as if she were daft.

"And for my prowess you should be more than willing to give me your time. Please, just listen to my story! I promise I will pay you handsomely for your time!"

As her eyes met his, Eden began to feel hope seep from her. At her impassioned plea there was no softening in his chiseled features, or in his stony gaze. In a final attempt she gave him her most imploring look, and then instantly regretted it, for the light in his eyes suddenly burned brighter. It was as if he knew her game.

"State your business," O'Connor bit out.

"I need you to find my twin brother."

Shane frowned. "You have a twin?"

"Yes I do."

God help the world, he thought.

He leaned to crush out his cheroot, his gaze watching

her with a burning, probing intensity. "*Why* do you need me to find your twin?"

"Because he's missing, of course," she said in a mildly exasperated voice.

Shane brought his thumb and forefinger up to knead the bridge of his nose. "*Why*, do you need me to find him? *Why* do you think he is missing, and not on some drunken spree entertaining the . . . uh . . . 'ladies'?"

"Well, Mr. O'Connor, that's very astute of you—excuse me, do you have a headache, sir?"

"Not yet."

Eden hurried on. "Actually I might agree with you that Philip could be on a drunken spree, but the circumstances surrounding his disappearance don't match that observation."

Shane lifted a brow.

"You see, Philip *does* spend a good deal of time in the brothels, and there are three in particular that he frequents. But the madames of all of them told me they haven't seen him for several days."

Shane gave her a strange look. "You went into a brothel?"

"No. I went into *three*. And Philip wasn't in any of them." She thought she caught the tiniest flicker of amusement in his silver eyes, then quickly dismissed the notion. Unlikely the man had a drop of mirth in him.

"What do you mean by 'the circumstances matching the observation'?"

Eden suddenly realized she had not produced a shred of evidence. "Please turn around and look away from me Mr. O'Connor."

"Like hell."

Though her heart thudded hard, Eden smiled radiantly. "But you must! You have to!"

"I don't *have* to do anything I don't damn well please, madame."

"Please, Mr. O'Connor." Her tearing eyes betrayed her guise of confidence. "I-I brought some evidence I think might help you with the case—that is if you take it. But it's—I had to carry it under my skirt. Please," she begged softly.

Faintly amused, Shane shifted his gaze out toward the bay. Out of the corner of his eye he saw her twirl around, hoist her layers of petticoats to her waist, and fumble with something.

She turned around again, and with a dramatic flair that was completely artless, she opened the chamois bag she had tied to the waistband of her pantalets. She grabbed his hand and plopped a huge, uncut diamond into the center of his palm. Then she took hold of his other hand and plunked down another stone—an extraordinary grass-green emerald as large as the enormous diamond.

"Where," he asked in a hard drawl, "did you get these?"

"That," Eden said, "is what I've come to tell you."

OFFICIAL RULES

To enter the sweepstakes below carefully follow all instructions found elsewhere in this offer.

The **Winners Classic** will award prizes with the following approximate maximum values: 1 Grand Prize: $26,500 (or $25,000 cash alternate); 1 First Prize: $3,000; 5 Second Prizes: $400 each; 35 Third Prizes: $100 each; 1,000 Fourth Prizes: $7.50 each. Total maximum retail value of Winners Classic Sweepstakes is $42,500. Some presentations of this sweepstakes may contain individual entry numbers corresponding to one or more of the aforementioned prize levels. To determine the Winners, individual entry numbers will first be compared with the winning numbers preselected by computer. For winning numbers not returned, prizes will be awarded in random drawings from among all eligible entries received. Prize choices may be offered at various levels. If a winner chooses an automobile prize, all license and registration fees, taxes, destination charges and, other expenses not offered herein are the responsibility of the winner. If a winner chooses a trip, travel must be complete within one year from the time the prize is awarded. Minors must be accompanied by an adult. Travel companion(s) must also sign release of liability. Trips are subject to space and departure availability. Certain black-out dates may apply.

The following applies to the sweepstakes named above:

No purchase necessary. You can also enter the sweepstakes by sending your name and address to: P.O. Box 508, Gibbstown, N.J. 08027. Mail each entry separately. Sweepstakes begins 6/1/93. Entries must be received by 12/30/94. Not responsible for lost, late, damaged, misdirected, illegible or postage due mail. Mechanically reproduced entries are not eligible. All entries become property of the sponsor and will not be returned.

Prize Selection/Validations: Selection of winners will be conducted no later than 5:00 PM on January 28, 1995, by an independent judging organization whose decisions are final. Random drawings will be held at 1211 Avenue of the Americas, New York, N.Y. 10036. Entrants need not be present to win. Odds of winning are determined by total number of entries received. Circulation of this sweepstakes is estimated not to exceed 200 million. All prizes are guaranteed to be awarded and delivered to winners. Winners will be notified by mail and may be required to complete an affidavit of eligibility and release of liability which must be returned within 14 days of date on notification or alternate winners will be selected in a random drawing. Any prize notification letter or any prize returned to a participating sponsor, Bantam Doubleday Dell Publishing Group, Inc., its participating divisions or subsidiaries, or the independent judging organization as undeliverable will be awarded to an alternate winner. Prizes are not transferable. No substitution for prizes except as offered or as may be necessary due to unavailability, in which case a prize of equal or greater value will be awarded. Prizes will be awarded approximately 90 days after the drawing. All taxes are the sole responsibility of the winners. Entry constitutes permission (except where prohibited by law) to use winners' names, hometowns, and likenesses for publicity purposes without further or other compensation. Prizes won by minors will be awarded in the name of parent or legal guardian.

Participation: Sweepstakes open to residents of the United States and Canada, except for the province of Quebec. Sweepstakes sponsored by Bantam Doubleday Dell Publishing Group, Inc., (BDD), 1540 Broadway, New York, NY 10036. Versions of this sweepstakes with different graphics and prize choices will be offered in conjunction with various solicitations or promotions by different subsidiaries and divisions of BDD. Where applicable, winners will have their choice of any prize offered at level won. Employees of BDD, its divisions, subsidiaries, advertising agencies, independent judging organization, and their immediate family members are not eligible.

Canadian residents, in order to win, must first correctly answer a time limited, arithmetical skill testing question. Void in Puerto Rico, Quebec and wherever prohibited or restricted by law. Subject to all federal, state, local and provincial laws and regulations. For a list of major prize winners (available after 1/29/95): send a self-addressed, stamped envelope entirely separate from your entry to: Sweepstakes Winners, P.O. Box 517, Gibbstown, NJ 08027. Requests must be received by 12/30/94. DO NOT SEND ANY OTHER CORRESPONDENCE TO THIS P.O. BOX.

Don't miss these fabulous Bantam women's fiction titles on sale in September

• A WHISPER OF ROSES

by Teresa Medeiros, author of HEATHER AND VELVET

A tantalizing romance of love and treachery that sweeps from a medieval castle steeped in splendor to a crumbling Scottish fortress poised high above the sea. _____29408-3 $5.50/6.50 in Canada

• TENDER BETRAYAL

by Rosanne Bittner, author of OUTLAW HEARTS

The powerful tale of a Northern lawyer who falls in love with a beautiful plantation owner's daughter, yet willingly becomes the instrument of her family's destruction when war comes to the South. _____29808-9 $5.99/6.99 in Canada

• THE PAINTED LADY

by Lucia Grahame

"A unique and rare reading experience." —Romantic Times In the bestselling tradition of Susan Johnson comes a stunningly sensual novel about sexual awakening set in 19th-century France and England. _____29864-X $4.99/5.99 in Canada

• OREGON BROWN

by Sara Orwig, author of NEW ORLEANS

A classic passionate romance about a woman forced to choose between fantasy and reality. _____56088-3 $4.50/5.50 in Canada